The Civil War is over, the sun continues to rise and life goes on. People return home and take up their old life or build a new one.

Emmanuel has a secret that must be kept at all costs; life depends upon it. But friends are gone, and people who understand are few. Is life even worth living?

Mina is free... or is she? She is a black woman in a world of white men. Law and society are neither blind nor fair, and too many look at her as no more than an object. It doesn't matter that she is a splendid cook, loved by a child and a devoted husband.

Johan can no longer be the man of war; the law frowns upon life by the sword. He has to learn how to build instead of destroy. More importantly, he must learn that every life has value, maybe even his own.

Hard work is ignored as often as rewarded. Thousands of good people flock to the lands of Minnesota hoping to build better lives for themselves and their children. But life on the frontier has always been cheap and hard, and where good people go those who would profit from them follow.

Men and women of flesh and blood, with Iron Conviction, is what it takes to make a life worth living.

IRON
CONVICTION

SHANE CHRISTEN

Seanchaí
Publications
CANNON FALLS MN

Published by Seanchaí Publications in 2022
First edition; First printing

Content © 2022 Shane Christen
Photography © 2012 Marie McNamara. Used with permission

ISBN 978-1-945105-00-5

To those who have read my first and asked me what happens next. To my sister who insisted I needed another editor, my friend Ellen who said 'no problem,' and to the neighbor who said "I like Johan; he's an SoB but he's my kind of SoB." Thank you.

Table of Contents

Johan looked across the table at the Colonel looking back at him. A Captain writing in a ledger sat beside the Colonel, the man looked so clean. Johan stood at attention waiting for the Colonel to speak. The room was sparse, not what he expected the office of a Colonel to look like. In all his years in various armies he had only a few times been called in to speak to a Colonel. Colonel Vienot had been a great man and a well-liked officer of the Legion. That had been when he was selected to learn to use a rifle. Then he had been asked by Colonel Sanborn to join the Regiment as part of the NCO cadre. Again, at Fort Abercrombie when the post Colonel had discovered his entire stock of whiskey had been issued out as a liquor ration. An unintentional smirk crossed Johan's face momentarily as he remembered that rather uncomfortable interview.

The Regiment had arrived yesterday in preparation to muster out. The First Sergeant had ordered him to report to the Colonel and this staff ass writing in the ledger from

God only knew where. Johan was trying to think of what he had done lately that might garner the attention of a Colonel.

The Colonel winced as he shifted in his chair. The wound he had received at Allatoona Pass still pained him. He was not alone in that. Several of the men in the ranks still suffered from wounds received during the war. Physical and mental wounds would plague most for the rest of their lives.

The Colonel looked down at the ledger in front of him then to the Captain beside him. "At ease Sergeant. I need to ask you some questions.

I'm told you have been taught to read. Is that correct?"

"Yes Sir." Johan replied with some pride as he settled into parade rest.

"I'm curious, what did they use to teach you?" The Colonel asked.

"Sir, Blackstone and Plutarch." Johan said as he felt his chest swell with pride.

The Colonel shook his head in amusement. "No one in their right mind would use the Bible on you."

"No Sir, the Captain was worried I might burst into flame," Johan said.

While the Colonel and the Captain beside him both chuckled. Johan knew the Captain had been half serious. The man had never wanted an out-of-control fire in his camp.

The Colonel shook his head in amusement. "What men from your company might you suggest for a career in the Army?"

Johan blinked in surprise. He hadn't expected that question. He tilted his head in thought; he had not expected that line of questioning at all. It took him only a few moments to gather a list in his mind. It was a short list.

"Sir, William Young is the first name that comes to mind. He is young and intelligent with ambition. He is also brave and honest to a fault. He has spoken of the wish to become an officer. He might make a good one.

Also, Seth Barnaby, he is very honest and has a good heart. Last year he spoke of possibly volunteering for service in one of the Colored Regiments. Though, I think that he has changed his mind since then and all he wishes is to see his family.

The rest of the men in my Company I think wish to return home and take up their lives where they left them as well. I can think of no others."

The Colonel looked hard at him. "Your Captain also mentioned Emmanuel Lentsch and you as likely candidates for the Regular Army. Is he wrong in such a suggestion?"

Johan again considered how to respond. "Sir, Emmanuel went off his head when his copain was killed at Allatoona Pass. Given the choice he will kill, I fear he may have come to enjoy it. I do not believe he has the temperament of a professional soldier. In all honesty sir, unless in battle I do not believe I would wish to serve beside him. It would become difficult to control his hate and point him in the right direction."

The Colonel nodded his head in understanding. "I suspect we will be fighting the plains Indians soon enough and he would get a belly full of fighting."

"Sir, the copain of Emmanuel today is Little Foot, the young Dakota man Sergeant Webb and I had to keep from taking scalps. In such a fight Emmanuel would have some very hard choices to make."

The Colonel gave Johan a long look and seemed to consider before he spoke. "And you, Sergeant? What about you?"

Johan had given some thought to the subject and had to think for a moment how to best express his view. A career in the Regular army was a possibility for a man like him but he thought such would be wrong for Mina and for her adopted child Freedom.

"Sir, I believe I am done with the life of a soldier. I think I will stay in Minnesota and become a barkeep."

The Colonel raised an eyebrow. "I know your penchant for finding liquor, but a barkeep? The Army needs experienced men like you. You would go far."

Johan shook his head and noticed the young Captain staring at him wrinkling his brow as if in deep thought. The man was so clean and seemed young but a Captain already. The yellow piping showed him to be of the cavalry and the revolver at his hip had a visibly well-worn butt that had clearly seen some hard use. His cheeks were sunken and his face bore the look of a man long under the sun. There was a vague familiarity to the man but Johan could not place him. He had seen many officers throughout the war, likely this had been one.

"Excuse me Colonel." The Captain said. "I believe the Sergeant and I have met. Sergeant Steele … did you trade in the Dakota Territory before the war?"

Johan looked at the Captain again trying to place him. "Sir, I did. I traded pots and pans for buffalo robes and did well enough."

The Captain nodded his head and looked to the Colonel. "I came across this man on my first command. A small expedition to the Dakota Territory to find some white children who had been stolen by savages."

Johan felt his jaw tighten and he spoke before thinking. "Sir, they are no more savages than I. You never found them, did you?"

The Captain flushed slightly. "No, Sergeant, I did not. We never had the pleasure of encountering any hostiles."

"Sir, your horses and men were tired. Had you encountered the hostiles I traded with you would not be here today."

The Captain furrowed his brow and the Colonel smiled slightly. "Where would I be, Sergeant?" the Captain asked.

"Sir, you would be dead with your scalp decorating a lance or lodge pole." Johan said simply. As soon as Johan spoke, he knew he should have kept his mouth shut.

The Captain started to rise from his chair. "Just what does that mean, Sergeant?" the Captain demanded through clenched teeth.

Johan winced and looked to the Colonel. "Sir… I do not know how to respond to the Captain."

The Colonel smiled again. "Just answer honestly, Sergeant."

Johan nodded. "Sir, you were young and foolish. The men you would have faced were hardened warriors. You had some good soldiers among your command, but they would have been outclassed. It would have been a fight; but a short one I think."

The Colonel smiled slightly and snorted his agreement. He spoke before the Captain could say anything. "Is that why you don't want to join the Regular Army? With your experience I can see you as a First Sergeant and likely working your way into the rank of Sergeant Major, especially if you were to transfer into a Colored Regiment."

The Captain tapped the table irritably. "Or are you too fond of the savages?"

Again, Johan paused to consider carefully how to answer before he spoke then he directed his answer at the Colonel.

"Sir, before the War I traded with the Lakota and their Cheyenne allies. I was most impressed with them as fighting men. I have fought the Cossack, Kabyle, Tuareg and other great horsemen. I would consider none the equal of the Lakota or Cheyenne. They will fight, and fight hard, but in the end, they will lose. I do not think the United States will be the better for it.

"I am tired of war and fighting. I wish to read a book beside a fire with a glass of cognac in my hand."

The Captain snorted in contempt. "Those savages don't hold a candle to men like Wheeler and Forrest."

The Colonel smiled and let out a slight laugh. "Captain, I suspect the Sergeant here would disagree. I might as well."

That comment abruptly silenced the Captain. "Sergeant, you were the Brigade hangman for two years and helped to train up a Regiment I consider among the finest fighting men of the Army of the Tennessee. Men like you, soldiers like you, will shape the future of the Army and this country. I would like nothing better than to see you and your wife occupying the NCO quarters at some army post I command."

Now it was Johan's turn to smile and shake his head. "Sir, I have fought wars on three continents. I have fought beside and against some of the finest soldiers to ever stand the line. When I came to America, I thought my days as a soldier were behind me; I was wrong. I had one more war in me. I am tired and too worn to be a good soldier much longer. I think I will do no more soldiering in this lifetime."

The Colonel straightened his back and reached up to rub his neck muscles. He stretched his neck trying to work a kink loose. "You know Sergeant, it won't be the same as the army. Civilians won't understand what you have seen or done. You're not going to be able to relate to them or them to you. You're going to be a stranger in a strange land wondering what the hell happened.

"Sergeant, you are a soldier and a damned fine one from what I know. Men like you don't know how to be anything else. Should you change your mind I think the US Army is the place for you. It would be a real shame if you died in bed instead of with a rifle in hand."

Post-Civil War Minnesota, 1865

Post Civil War Minnesota was the frontier of a rapidly expanding United States. Land was available and inexpensive. Minnesota had suffered badly during the Dakota War, with large swaths of land completely abandoned to the Dakota. Many settlers never returned. Opportunity abounded. Those willing to work hard could make a future there.

*S*eth took a deep breath and stopped; he looked up the hill at the two pine trees framing the road as it crossed the ridgeline. This curve in the road was so familiar that he knew how many and what kind of trees lined the road. His father had planted many of them. Below the road in the creek they used to fish and hunt squirrels. They all knew exactly where the best place to perch and watch the homestead from the hill was. The house was just over the crest ahead, not even a half mile. He was home.

Seth looked back at the little column behind him. Mrs. Mina with her black hair tied back into a tight braid was driving the mule cart. Little Miss Freedom sat in a big basket on the seat beside her. Mina was wearing a nicely broken in army dress hat and a new blue dress that Sergeant Steele had bought her in Washington City, with her hair tied back in a tight braid. Her dark eyes looked at him from her pretty face and she smiled slightly. She knew they were almost home.

Striding beside the cart were Emmanuel and Little Foot; Sergeant Steele was off somewhere in that creek bed. Emmanuel looked so strange not wearing an army sack coat, but his bedroll was over his left shoulder with the new Spencer rifle he had bought in Washington City slung over his right. A nice new broad brimmed black hat framed his short cut blonde hair. He hadn't had that new hat a day before he tossed it on the ground and stomped it flat, then reshaped it to his liking. It fit him better now. Seth wished Emmanuel would smile again, play the fiddle with the enthusiasm that he used to, before Nate had been killed.

18

Everyone missed Nate; it was hard not to. There were so many others gone now, buried in the southland. Sebastian, Allen, too many other young lives gone forever. The survivors would bear the physical scars of the war for the rest of their lives. Seth shook his head; that was not the kind of thing to dwell upon today. He was home!

Little Foot was stripped to the waist with his Springfield slung over his shoulder, his black hair framing his dark square featured face. He had sold his new army brogans as soon as he mustered out and made himself a set of moccasins before he had left Ft. Snelling. His bedroll rode on the back of the blue roan pony tied behind the cart. It was hot and Little Foot looked comfortable with his muscular bare chest exposed to the breeze. The sun and four years a soldier had grown him into a man. Seth remembered how small he had seemed when he had first seen him but now, he rippled with the lean powerful muscles of the runner who had marched to the sea and home to Minnesota via Washington City.

Sergeant Steele stepped onto the road from the creek bed; he must have washed his face and hands, as water glistened in his beard. There had always been quite a lot of salt and pepper in that beard, but it was more salt than pepper now. He was wearing the same uniform he had been discharged in. The man looked the same as he had on any day in the army. He still wore the stripes on his sleeve and wore the uniform like he belonged in it. The Whitney rifle in his hands was the same he had carried through most of the war. He was even still wearing all of his leathers and the vicious sabre bayonet that had saved Seth's life, as well as carrying canteen, haversack and blanket roll. Almost everyone else had shed their uniforms

19

at the first opportunity, but not Sergeant Steele. Looking at the man you wouldn't know he was just out of the army.

Steele stopped beside him, slung his rifle and fished his pipe and bag of tobacco out of his coat pocket. He motioned with his chin towards the house. "Your home is just there," he said as he packed his pipe.

Seth felt a grin cross his face. "The top of the ridge is the edge of our land. We're not much more than a half mile from the house."

"You are certain you wish the four of us to winter with you?" Sergeant Steele asked.

"Oh, I don't know what I'd do without you all this winter. I wish Bryce and Kevin would have come."

But the Sergeant shook his head. "Bryce wished to get back to his Great Lake and to the life of a sailor. Kevin is in town and planning to make a start as a gunsmith. I expect they will both do well."

Mrs. Mina chose that moment to pull the cart up beside them and stop. "Afraid the farm is gone?" She asked with a smile.

Seth laughed, then stopped and removed his own hat to run a hand through his hair. "I just... I don't know. I just need to prepare myself to see my family."

Little Foot and Emmanuel stopped beside them. Both had cheap white clay penny pipes in their mouths. Sergeant Steele struck a Lucifer on the striker of his match safe and lit both of their pipes. Their little group of five blocked the road completely. Seth found himself studying the surrounding woods and hills out of habit. He shook his head in annoyance; the war was over.

There were no rebels here, and according to his sister's letters, not a hostile Indian within two hundred miles. But it was a habit picked up from four years of war. He noted that both Little Foot and Emmanuel had done the same thing and he chuckled to himself as he realized Sergeant Steele had only come back to the road after he was certain there were no threats within range of his rifle.

Seth smiled again. "I just can't believe the war is really over. The army is in the past, no more hardtack and salt horse." After a deep breath he added, "I can sleep in my own bed again."

Sergeant Steele exhaled a cloud of smoke and scratched his beard. "It will be uncomfortable for a while. You are used to sleeping on the ground." His tone was quiet, but definite; the voice of experience.

Little Foot grunted. "I hate sleeping on a bed. I never will again."

Emmanuel looked at him like he was a little mad. "Can we just go? I want some coffee and to sit down on a chair instead of a rock or a log. I wouldn't mind putting my feet under a real table for supper either. The way you've been bragging up your mother and sister, I expect something good in my stomach tonight."

Emmanuel looked into the basket turned into child's bed that held Little Miss Freedom. Seth stepped closer for a look as well. The child was sleeping peacefully with her precious turtle shell rattle gripped tightly to her chest. A slight smile graced her tiny face. It was hard to believe the child had been with them almost a year now. She couldn't have been too much older than that. She was the same shade as Mrs. Mina, with hair that was considerably lighter and wilder. Her eyes were as black as pitch and always alive with mischief. She was already standing and almost walking. She loved it when Emmanuel played his fiddle for her and would stand and try to dance. Seth expected her to be running before long.

"Let's go, I've been looking forward to seeing your sister," Mrs. Mina said with a smile and that slight southern drawl in her voice. "I can't wait for her to meet Freedom."

Seth felt a shiver slide down his back as he remembered the scene in that clearing where they had found Little Miss Freedom. A shudder shook his whole body as he turned towards home. The war was over, such scenes were forever behind him now. He had to keep telling himself that and he constantly prayed nothing like that would ever happen again.

Seth absently reached up and scratched the jagged bayonet scar on his neck. His toes curled in his shoes as he looked forward to the feel of his bare feet on the horse-hair rug in front of the fireplace. There would be fresh sourdough bread at home and his stomach growled in eager expectation.

As he crested the ridgeline, he saw the homestead. It was just as he had remembered. He could see someone hanging out laundry. Even at the best part of a half mile he knew it was Carlie. He had so badly wanted to introduce Sebastian to her. But his name graced the rolls of the fallen, and she had written of meeting a veteran who had already mustered out, though she had been scant with the details.

Smoke rose from the chimney on the summer kitchen and there was a new woodpile between the house and the pole shed they had built the winter before the war. Someone had simply offloaded several wagons worth of wood into a pile instead of stacking it into wind breaks. Seth shook his head. One of the first tasks would be to fix that. He felt a tear start down his cheek. He was home, something none of the others with him could say.

Little Foot had no idea where his people were, Emmanuel flatly refused to speak of his family and Sergeant Steele and Mrs. Mina had no home yet. They were all planning to head west in the spring to a place Sergeant Steele had seen before the war, and again when they were based at Fort Abercrombie. Seth wished they would settle nearer but he understood; none were all that fond of people, and people were fairly scarce that far west.

Seth wiped away the tear and tried to think of an appropriate bible passage. Nothing came to mind. All he could think of was the mealtime prayer.

He lowered his head and quietly gave the only prayer that came to mind. "Bless us, oh Lord, and these thy gifts which we are about to receive. And for thy bounty; through Christ our Lord. Amen." Or, was it from thy bounty? He shook his head, it didn't matter. He was home; the war was over. His dream of a peaceful life raising horses was at hand.

Johan hung back and watched his little cavalcade enter the farmyard. A breeze kicked up just as the women of the house exploded from the house like a cannon shot. They rushed to hug Seth then surrounded Mina and Freedom. They at least acknowledged Emmanuel and looked askance at Little Foot but the women were there for Seth, Mina and the baby; they needed no distractions.

After the Dakota War Johan knew an Indian was not likely to receive a warm welcome anywhere in Minnesota. He was pleasantly surprised when Seth's mother gave Little Foot a strong hug and from the startled expression that crossed his dark face so was Little Foot. A couple of children that must have been Seth's cousins emerged from the barn leading a pony. As soon as they saw Seth they pushed it into the corral and sprinted flat out to the cart tackling him to the ground.

The entire yard erupted in joyful laughter as Seth rolled on the ground with the children tickling them furiously. A pair of women looked on from the porch. The younger one had sad eyes and looked about to cry. The older horse faced woman stared at the group in as obviously disapproving a manner as she could.

Johan felt an instant dislike for the old woman. He was not certain how she was related, but knew she must be the high-born aunt Seth had spoken of. Her face was tight squeezed with small eyes that stared hatefully at the group. He wasn't sure if she was glaring at Little Foot or Mina. Neither of them seemed to have noticed, or gave any sign they cared if they had. There was just too much joy around them for a sour look to spoil their mood.

Johan walked up beside the blue roan tied behind the cart. Little Foot had bought the horse in St Paul and Johan could see it was a good horse. He ran his fingers through the mane. The horse nudged him in appreciation looking for a treat and Johan just stood there watching others as he had his entire life. He had witnessed homecomings before but had never received one. His whole life had been that of an outsider looking in, and it did not bother him that today was no different. He did not expect a joyful homecoming. Nor did he did not begrudge those who received it either; especially when they so clearly deserved it. Seth certainly appreciated it, and no one seemed to mind when Carlie wrapped Mina in a tight hug as tears of joy streamed down both their lovely faces. Mina smiled broadly, half lifting Carlie off her feet to spin her in a circle.

Johan smiled at the happiness in front of him. Not even the hateful stare of the horse faced aunt could lessen this moment. Seth was home and was the man of the house. And he was indeed a man full-grown now; the youth that had left four years ago was gone, replaced by a man forged in the fires of war.

Seth's mother stepped around the cart and looked at him. Tears of joy streamed down her face. She had aged in the four years since he had last seen her. Crow's feet framed her eyes and gray dominated her hair. The constant worry of losing her only son had clearly told upon her. but through the war years had not been kind, she was still a handsome woman. She looked at Johan a moment and turned to Mina asking a question he did not hear.

She nodded at whatever Mina said and walked to him in three long steps. When she stopped in front of him it was so abrupt that Johan took a step back, half expecting a slap, though he had no idea what he might have done to deserve on. At least, not lately. She smiled and pursed her lips. She looked back at Mina again who was holding a grinning Freedom then back to Johan.

"You brought my son back to me... I can never thank you enough," she said around her joy and threw her arms around him in a tight hug that startled Johan.

At first, he was unsure if he should return the hug. Then he set his rifle against the cart and hugged her back. It was far from appropriate, but he did not care. She stepped back and looked him up and down, wiping her tears away as she did so.

"Seth wrote that you and Mina were coming and bringing a baby you had adopted in the southland. He says that you'll head west in the spring.

"You don't have to. The three of you can stay as long as you like. The room above the well house is ready for your little family. And your other two friends can stay in the carriage house."

Johan looked at her, not sure how he should respond. He had no wish to be rude or to fail to show enough appreciation for what she was offering. "No, we will stay through the winter. Mina and I wish to build a business. An inn and tavern where Mina can bake her bread and feed the weary travelers."

She smiled. "You might build such a business in town."

"Too many people for me. I prefer the west, I think," Johan said carefully. "I think that would be better for all of us."

"Oh, but..." Then joy left her face as she turned slightly to glance at the horse-faced aunt, and looked back at Mina and Little Foot. "I see. Yes. You're quite right."

Mina held Freedom to her chest and looked at the room they had been given for the winter. It was as snug and comfortable as she remembered. It had not sat unused in the years since she had last slept here. The bed had been moved so that any breeze from the open window swept the bed. Someone had also swept the floor and cleaned the window recently.

Johan had already brought his bedroll and her camp chest in and set it at the foot of the bed. She looked over at the small table with a water pitcher and wash basin and noticed that he had set her small mirror and comb there. It was a little thing she appreciated.

Mina moved to the window and looked down at the space between the well house and main house. Carlie was there sweeping dust out of the summer kitchen. Mina turned her head and could see Johan and Seth splitting wood from the large woodpile and stacking it beside the house to form a windbreak.

The rhythmic sound of a splitting maul was pleasing to her ears, but something was missing. She paused to try and discern what it could be. The realization that there was no smell of cook fires, or the sound of hundreds of soldiers going about their daily routine, made her take in a deep breath. There was no stink of open latrines and unwashed men, either; and Mina was not going to miss that scent. There was also no worry of guerillas or a rebel army appearing on the horizon. The war was over, peace and freedom were at hand. There would never again be the need to worry about anyone asking to see her emancipation papers. Freedom was as real as the child named after it. Mina had thought about burning those papers but decided against it. That simple piece of paper with Johan's signature was as good as any marriage license. He could have simply taken her but had instead set her free, given her a choice.

Mina knew she was bound to Johan. She didn't mind, he was her man. She had chosen him to be her husband. He hadn't ever taken advantage of or used her; he treated her better than many she had seen. The money she earned was hers; he never claimed it. In fact, he never mentioned it. There was no doubt that he was her man, though. He didn't visit the houses of ill repute or wander off to some other woman. Mina knew there had been men who had suffered at his hands because they had slighted or spoke ill of her, and she suspected at least one man might have even died for it.

The bed beckoned her and she moved to it, remembering the first time she had invited Johan into hers. He had simply crawled under the covers and went to sleep. She looked forward to his gentle touch tonight. The thought of his rough fingers gently caressing her face brought a smile to her lips.

Mina looked down at the blanket stretched across the top. There was no US sewn into the center. She had grown used to army issue blankets and liked the US that she had come to think of as meaning "us." She could see that the ropes under the straw pallet were tight and laid Freedom down next to the pillow at the head of the bed. Freedom looked so tin,y sleeping comfortably and loosely wrapped in her blanket.

Mina had no idea where Johan had gotten that blanket but the crushed red velvet was soft and perfect for Freedom. The tiny baby squirmed and murmured in her sleep; she wasn't really a baby anymore. Mina swept an errant lock of hair from her own face and just stood there staring down at Freedom. That little girl was her daughter; and she was a mother now, with all the responsibilities that came with motherhood.

Mina saw her reflection in the small silver framed mirror. That image was so different from the frightened young woman Johan had found in Charleston. She had a family now. A husband and daughter, not to mention a mess of men who looked at her the same way that she expected they looked at their own sisters and mothers.

She looked out the window and realized Emmanuel and Little Foot were above the carriage house setting their paltry possessions. Little Foot had little more than his new bought horse and what he carried.

Emmanuel had little more than that; a fiddle, as well as a few small hand tools in a leather roll so that he might make more instruments if he chose. Though she was rather certain Emmanuel had a good amount of money set aside. Other than a new hat, set of clothes, and the Spencer rifle, he hadn't bought much with his pay.

Little Foot would never fit in here, and his chances of making a life were not good if he stayed. She could never forget him telling Johan that he needed to be told which white men he was to kill as they all looked the same to him. He was an Indian; and even though he had a white man's name when he wanted to use it, he obviously never would. He didn't want to be a white man.

Emmanuel was still broken by the loss of his 'copain' Nate. So cold and full of rage. He almost never smiled anymore, unless he was playing with Freedom. He had spent a large part of the march to the sea and through the Carolinas actively hunting rebels. Johan had told her he had shot at and likely killed several of Wheeler's men and a few militia and patty rollers that had gotten too close to his sights. Then he had volunteered for every forage party, likely hoping to encounter the enemy. Mina had no doubt he had become a proficient arsonist as well. Not the sort of man she was really comfortable around; she preferred the man Emmanuel had been before Nate had been killed at Allatoona Pass.

Mina sat down on the bed beside Freedom running her hands along the blanket smoothing a crease in the wool. She had slept so long on a pallet or a scrap lumber bed the men had hammered together for her and the other laundresses that this felt like a slice of heaven. She closed her eyes and lay all the way down spreading her arms wide and let out a sigh that the good Lord himself must have smiled at.

A New Home

Working from dawn to dusk could create great works. But it was hard work to build a future from the wilderness.

Dynamite is invented by Alfred Nobel, and the U.S. passes the first Civil Rights Act.

Emmanuel woke with a start, drenched in a cold sweat, and wiped Nate's blood and brains from his face. It took a few moments of silence to come fully awake and realize he was in a bed, not in the mud and blood of a nightmare. The war was over, he knew it, but it still took the mind time to grasp that reality, and everyone dealt with that grasping in their own way. In his case the nightmares and memories were still too close.

Emmanuel got out of bed and crossed to the small table beside the window. The floor was uneven but oddly soft on his bare feet. He poured a healthy bit of water into the wash basin and splashed his face. The cold water brought him fully awake and chased away the image of life being snatched from his best friend; a boy he had loved like a little brother. He didn't realize he was scrubbing his hands raw until he felt a trickle of blood. He stopped and stood there staring at the wooden slats that covered the beams of the wall.

One of the mules in the stable below the room brayed loudly and it startled him. He looked down at his nightshirt and realized just how drenched in sweat it was. He shook his head in annoyance and looked out the window at the yard. He had a good view of the front of the tavern, the recessed entry of the door, the yard and the small clearing to the east they were using for a pasture.

Those walls were the best part of three feet thick and of some local stone that had come from just across the road. The way the tavern was built into the side of the hill it would be cool in the heat of summer and the way Johan had set the fireplace and pot-bellied stove it would stay warm enough in the winter. Emmanuel half expected to sleep in the tavern during the coldest part of winter since there wasn't a stove in this room yet. One had been ordered from the new dry goods store in town, but no one was sure when it would arrive.

Four windows and two doors were visible from this side of the building and almost one more door into the bakery and inn on the floor above that he could just see from the window. The wood was all locally sourced as well. Johan had hired several men to help build the place. All had done good work with axe and adze. The first building up had been the well house and stable with this room above and then the outhouse. It really was more of a palace as such structures went. Johan had taken a running iron and with the assistance of Mrs. Mina, to make certain of the proper spelling, had burned 'Enlisted' into one door and 'Officers' into the other. The thought of that brought a smile to the face. No one could say the man didn't have at least some humor in him.

A traveling carpenter, Dale Hammond, had set his wagon across the road and traded a month of work for two twenty-dollar gold eagles, food and a bed in the inn. In exchange he made the bar, doors and furniture through-out the place. He was very skilled, his work simple, strong, and highly efficient, but not always very nice to look at. He wasted very little wood, only using metal hinges and latches on the entrance doors and window shutters. Emmanuel thought he had robbed them until he made the bar for the tavern. It was a piece of absolute beauty. Made from a single tree trunk, the bar had been shaped into a stunning work of art.

That he was a fellow veteran and doing a bit of a favor for Johan was part of it. Dale had been a pioneer in the Army of the Cumberland and been badly injured at Peachtree Creek when a caisson had rolled over him. It left him with a badly broken leg that he had been lucky not to have lost. Emmanuel could see that his wound pained him when when the days were cold or wet. He always limped, but the limp became more pronounced when it rained.

Emmanuel looked at the blood-tinged water in the basin and saw the eyes looking back at him. They were the eyes of Emma. The frightened young woman who had threatened to brain father with an axe if he ever raised a hand to her again. Father had been laughing until Emma picked up the axe…

If Emma were here, she might have thought Dale a handsome man. Dale was kind and fairly good looking in a wolfish sort of way. A hardworking man, with a kind manner and fair features who would make a good husband for some lucky maid. Emma certainly would have liked him.

Emmanuel looked up at the reflection in the glass of the window and smiled slightly. Emma had been rail thin with broad shoulders and thick wrists for a woman. Some of his earliest memories had been Emma using a froe to make kindling. Then as she grew into it, father taught her to use a maul to split the firewood. Later father taught her the axe so she could help fell and trim trees. Then he would haul it to town and sell it a wagonload at a time.

The last time Emma's father had raised a hand to her she had finally had enough and threatened to split his skull if he hit her again. He hadn't taken her seriously until she raised the axe. Emma had disappeared that night; Emmanuel had buried her bloody dress in the woods not far from the shack.

The war started a month later, and Emmanuel had rushed to join to stay as far from father as possible. Very few people from town knew him. Some knew Emma but she had always worn hand me down clothes a few sizes too large. Her hips and bust had never been much for anyone to look at anyway. No one missed her enough to look for her, which likely saved her father from a neck stretching.

After the first time her father had grabbed her by the hair Emma had shorn her hair short and never let it grow back. She had never been pretty or been all that interested in boys. Too many were likely to be like father, and the rest didn't seem all that bright. She had never really known their mother and had never had anyone to teach her how a woman was to act. Father's influence hadn't helped that much either.

Father had pushed Emma to go to school for three years. That had been enough to learn to read and write some and to know the numbers and figures. It was there that Emma learned she had an ear for music and some natural skill with the fiddle.

The little cabin they grew up in hadn't been a lot bigger than an officer's tent, but it had been ample for them. Emmanuel understood now that Father had probably tried but had just not been suited to be a parent. He had a temper and would take his frustrations out on whatever or whoever was unlucky enough to be at hand. It certainly didn't help that he liked his beer.

The man had tried to be a father though. He really had. He had seen to it that Emma had more of an education than he ever had. He had also done his best to provide a roof over their heads, clothes and food in the belly. To think about it Emmanuel really didn't have any hatred towards him. Emma and Emmanuel just didn't give a damn one way or another if Father was dead or not.

To be honest, if someone were to ask, Emmanuel or Emma might look at Johan and Mrs. Mina as family or more likely the family anyone would wish they had.

Emmanuel loved Little Miss Freedom like she was a little sister and trusted and liked Mrs. Mina. It was only a wild guess how old Mrs. Mina was, but she was likely about the same age as Emmanuel. Johan was an absolute villain, a bastard of the highest order who would steal at the drop of a hat and whose morals when it came to life belonged nowhere near a church. And still Emmanuel would trust him with life and libert,y and had done so many times in the past.

There was only a half moon tonight... or this morning, rather, as it felt like dawn was on its way. The front of the tavern and yard were still illuminated by the moon. Emmanuel missed the sounds of an army camp; the snores, rustling of blankets and constant sound were oddly comforting. Silence seemed wrong somehow, but the peacefulness of that silence was close to heaven.

Emmanuel's brow furrowed. There was a faint glow by the door. Now what... He shook his head. The mind was awfully slow this morning; that glow was Johan's pipe. He was standing there in the shadow looking toward this window. Had Johan heard a scream from the nightmare? Had there been a scream? Did it even matter?

Emmanuel would often wonder if Johan knew the secret of Emma's death. There was always half a thought that he might, but Emmanuel had never been all that good at reading people. Only Nate had ever known the secret and that was because he had been their nearest neighbor. Nate had gone to school with Emma and had been the only one to play with her in the schoolyard.

Johan would do or say something that would convince Emmanuel that he was thoughtful and wise, only for him to later say something that would convince anyone listening that he was simple. All men were really that way.

Though Emmanuel had to admit Johan was a man of a different sort, one nobody had quite figured even after serving beside him across the war. The answer Johan had to most problems was to deal with it, kill it, or ignore it and hope it went away. The man was quick and decisive; sometimes too quick. While many often thought him a fool he really only rarely proved it.

They had arrived here late in the spring and spent the summer building everything up. Emmanuel hadn't expected or really understood just how much work there would be. There was a stake in the success of the place; a full quarter that Emmanuel had bought in. So, all had tucked right in to build the place. They had expanded and cleared the natural clearing enough for the buildings. Every tree they felled was either set aside for firewood or for some future building project.

During one of the patrols from Fort Abercrombie Johan had seen this place and a large bit of lumber that had been set aside for some project or another. That stack of lumber was still there when they arrived, which had been quite a surprise for everybody.

Johan had walled up the spring and set the foundations of the well house while Emmanuel had been felling trees. The water was good, flowing out of a split in the rock of the hillside. It took some time to make the cistern and plan for the overflow to fill a water trough that would be part of the stable. Everyone had been pleasantly surprised to see how well the arrangement worked when the building was completed.

Emmanuel was proud to have helped with almost every part of the construction process. It had mostly been manual labor but despite skill with an axe and froe, proficiency in the use of a spade, shovel, and adze were quickly acquired. Johan's friend Willy had done all of the mortise and tenon work as well as fixing many of the building design issues that came up during construction.

Willy had been in an Iowa Cavalry Regiment and still carried his Sharp's Carbine with him almost everywhere. He had arrived with a one-horse wagon and started work almost immediately. His tool chest didn't hold much more than a broad axe, saw, square, T auger, scribe and a set of dividers. He set his bedroll under his wagon every night. The man typically worked from sun up to sun down every day except Sunday when he would walk with Mrs. Mina and Freedom to the new little country church on the outskirts of town.

Emmanuel would have thought Willy was well into his sixties from his weathered face and salt and pepper beard but no one really knew. He had massive hands and shoulders as well as a quiet demeanor that all appreciated. As old as he might have been it was a devil of a time keeping up with Willy. He was contemplative and appreciative of the help anyone provided. There was also no doubt that he enjoyed Mrs. Mina's cooking. Then again, everyone but a fool did.

Emmanuel liked him all the more because he refused to share any of Johan's drink. The man preferred coffee or water. He had said he was planning to build a business in town. There was no doubt he could do it and would probably be a success.

Movement at the tavern door pulled Emmanuel from his scattered thoughts. Johan had stepped onto the dirt path and knocked his spent pipe tobacco out on the bottom of his boot. He looked up at the window and waved as he turned back to the tavern. He was either up early or sleeping in the tavern again instead of in the tent with Mrs. Mina and Freedom.

They hoped to finish the roof by mid-day so Mrs. Mina and Freedom could move in permanently, but Emmanuel questioned that. The wagon with the cedar shingles hadn't arrived yet.

When that roof was finished Willy would be done. Dale would be gone a month after that and with Little Foot long gone to the west there would only be Johan, Mrs. Mina and Freedom. Everyone else was gone. Not that such was really all that bothersome.

Mina stepped away from the fire and wiped her hands. The army oven Johan had built would be a godsend in the summer and she could use the oven he had bought in the tavern in the winter which would help heat the place. She was tired and needed a few minutes to herself. Freedom was sitting quietly in her basket seeing what was going on around her and seemed intent on watching Johan working on the stone wall of the lean to at the moment.

That little girl particularly loved to watch Willy work. Whenever he did his mortise and tenon work she had to see and would get excited when he brought out his dividers to verify his work.

Willy had made quite the impression on Freedom. The first day Willy had started work here Freedom had been particularly cranky and more than a little loud. Mina had set a screaming Freedom in her basket and walked away, otherwise she was afraid she might lose her calm. Willy had stepped up and picked Freedom up and with a smile said: 'I don't believe it; I just don't believe it!'

Freedom had been so startled to be handled by a stranger that she went silent a moment then got ready a proper exercise of her lungs. Mina had thought he had only made matters worse until he used that startled silence to tickle Freedom with a feather and to play with her. It had worked like she never could have expected and now Freedom loved to simply watch Willy work and would bounce up and down in excitement whenever she saw him approach to play with her or to hand her a simple wooden toy. She had a cow, a stone top that Willy called a plumb bob, and a small wooden hammer which she refused to let go of. The turtle shell rattle that was her favorite never left her side, but that little Freedom-sized hammer was almost always clenched in her tiny fist. All too often it was being brandished to make a point.

Mina thought Freedom was too small for her age but no one else seemed to agree. What everyone did note was how that little girl seemed to always be watching everything with those big dark eyes. She seemed to take note of anything that was going on around her; she screamed only when she had dirty nappies or was going through a growth spurt.

Freedom was normally quiet and Mina was sure she was highly intelligent. Having a child around was far more work than she ever imagined. Mina hadn't been around children very much since she was a child herself. Freedom had been an eye-opening experience. Thankfully the other laundresses who weren't supposed to be with the Brigade and more than a few experienced fathers had helped.

General Sherman had decreed that no laundresses, sick men or non-essentials were to attend the march to Savannah. But it would have taken hell itself to keep her away. Johan had said nothing and the Captain and other officers had only smiled. They knew what their orders were worth where she was concerned. No one, not a single man had complained about her presence and at the last pay call she had received a teamsters pay for driving the regimental supply wagon. How that got past the Colonel she had no idea, and she hadn't complained about the extra money.

Mina stood there next to the tavern and inn Johan and Emmanuel had built with the help from just four men. Most of the work was done, all that was left was the roof shingles and some minor finish work inside. She liked the furniture that Dale had made. It was simple, robust and she expected it would weather the abuse of strangers rather well. The work Willy had done was incredible; what mistakes there were, if any, were not noticeable. At least not by her. She liked the look of the open rafters in the tavern and the main floor of the inn. The wide-open spaces made the rooms seem larger. The windows on the inn floor faced south and would provide ample light year around. With the way the tavern sat into the hill, heat from the room below would rise into the main floor of the inn helping to keep the rooms warm throughout the winter. The large windows on the main floor could be opened in the summer for the breeze and shuttered against the cold.

Dale was putting the finishing touches on a bed for her. It was the same size as the ones on the third floor, but Dale had carved some very pretty floral designs into her bed frame. Willy had found a hollowed-out stump in the woods and turned it into a swinging crib for Freedom. He had hung rope from a rafter and set the crib next to her bed so she could reach out with her hand or foot to rock it. He had even made some simple bookshelves for her. Right now, they only had a few books, maybe twenty total, but she planned to get more.

Johan was building a stone woodshed on the west side of the tavern that would provide both a dry space for wood and also led to the root cellar she had demanded be attached to the building. It was cut deep into the hillside and would stay cool through the summer and relatively warm in the winter.

Willy and Emmanuel sat a few yards to the right of her talking quietly. They were waiting for Johan to finish the last bit of wall so they could raise the last timbers for the lean-to roof.

"Emmanuel, any idea where Johan learned to work stone like that?" Willy asked appreciatively.

Mina tilted her head to listen, she had no idea where her Johan had learned such a thing either. She wondered if Emmanuel might know.

Emmanuel took off his hat and wiped his brow before answering. "It wouldn't have been in the army, we didn't do any stone work that I can remember. I know he traded out west with the Lakota before the war. So, maybe before he came to the US, probably with the French army. I think I remember him saying he had helped build roads in Africa."

Willy stroked his salt and pepper beard. "I sure am glad I don't speak French; I'm pretty sure I would be going straight to hell just for understanding the language he uses.

"He's doing a decent enough job with setting that stone, though. I suspect it will last. "

Mina understood that was quite the compliment coming from Willy. She had known he had been rather annoyed when he had first seen the crude plans she and Johan had presented to him. Willy had pointed out some mistakes and made some suggestions which Johan had adopted. He had said that a rough stone floor for the tavern was a bad idea but had watched in surprise when Johan dropped wheelbarrow after wheelbarrow of sand from the creek bed both underneath and over the top of the stone, sweeping the sand between stone slabs to create a fairly even floor. Willy had also been mightily impressed with the way Johan had used the mules to move those large pieces of stone from the hill above the creek on the other side of the road.

She was proud of her Johan. She didn't know where all the money came from, but it was there and with hers and what Emmanuel had put into the endeavor the place was built, paid for, and largely stocked. But it was going to be hard endless work even with Emmanuel helping.

She liked Dale and Willy but the other two not so much. Mark and Peter were local boys of seventeen or eighteen years, and she didn't really care for either of them. Both were young and 'full of piss and wind' as Johan said. They had been less than polite to her just once where Johan could hear, and he had set them straight quite bluntly.

While she didn't care for those two, she could not fault their work ethic. Every morning at sunup they were there and did everything they were told to do without complaint. After they had tasted her cooking they came to appreciate her and when she presented them with bear sign after the first week they complimented her at every opportunity.

She smiled at the memory of Willy and Dale looking at each other over the top of that plate of bear sign and telling her that if they knew donuts were going to be part of the pay they would have been here a week earlier. Dale had said if Johan died he would propose. Emmanuel hadn't taken that real well, but Johan had merely laughed and told Dale to get in line behind Emmanuel. He said that kind of thing often and likely believed it. She didn't.

Emmanuel worked as an assistant to Johan or Willy most of the time. Mina had to admit she was somewhat jealous of Emmanuel; he spent more time with Johan than she did. But she understood why; there was a look in Emmanuel's eyes that Johan understood and could relate to. Those eyes were dead now, void of emotion. Looking into his eyes was like looking into an empty glass. With his friend Little Foot gone west in a vain attempt to find his family, Emmanuel had grown more morose and distant. He rarely played his fiddle anymore except to entertain Freedom and had stopped working on the new one he had started to build at the Barnaby place.

Mina wished Little Foot had stayed instead of continuing west. She understood why he'd gone on, though. This part of Minnesota had seen too much of what they were calling the 'Dakota War' and no Indian was welcome.

Everyone there sat around the fire at night and talked. Some of it was what was going to happen the next day, some was recollections from the War or before. Freedom would sit beside Mina and just listen, almost always falling asleep against her side. She had always been very clingy, disliking being alone at all.

Johan had returned from town this afternoon with flour, coffee, sugar and some mail. Though there were no letters for Johan or Emmanuel there were two in the flowing hand of Carlie as well as a care package full of dried peaches for Dale from his family. Seth wrote Johan once a month and Johan only occasionally asked her for help with a word anymore. Though he would still often ask her for assistance with composing a reply. As he became a better reader that would stop and be one less thing that connected him to her. Johan always replied to those letters from Seth. As often as not it was news of Freedom and updates on how construction was proceeding.

Willy had spoken of a family in Iowa. Parents and three brothers farming somewhere. After the war he said he had developed a bit of the wander lust. He wanted to see what was on the other side of the next hill. That had lasted as far as the Dakota Territory where he had decided his scalp was worthwhile and headed back into Minnesota. She really liked the man and so did Johan. They had met at some point during the Vicksburg campaign and managed to remain in contact, though Mina had absolutely no idea how.

Life here at the crossroads would be good. There were neighbors just out of sight to the east and west as well as another some bit farther north on that road. The lake was a little less than a mile to the south where that road turned towards town. There was a small pond a little to the east of their place, she could just almost see it through the trees.

They were maybe an hour and a half walk from town, but she had no real want to go there except to church on Sundays. The dry goods store had a few books and fabric she could use to make clothing, but little else she wanted or needed. One of the drovers who had stopped and visited with Johan had mentioned there was to be a bookstore in town soon, but she would believe that when she saw it. The postmaster was a mean little man who would turn his back on her if she walked by or into the post office. Though he was very talkative and friendly when Johan was with her.

Their preacher had been a Chaplain during the war and gave superb sermons that she liked very much. His wife liked her and Freedom but seemed standoffish and overly moody towards everyone at times.

The neighbors to the west had just finished building a sod house. The two young girls were pretty and very nice. Their mother seemed off, and rarely spoke. She was a nice enough woman, but a lazy eye gave her an odd appearance. Her husband was ambitious and spoke longingly of the fields he would clear. But both Johan and Willy had said he had come too late in the season to do much more than build a house and cut firewood. Johan had called the man a fool for arriving here with three women to care for and little else. Mina had put Freedom on her hip and taken them a bag of bread and vegetables yesterday. Mr. Sipes had been using an ox to pull stumps from his field and his two girls had been using a felling axe to clumsily split wood. Their mother had seen her coming and disappeared into their little sod house. As Mina had arrived at the door, she had emerged with a faint smile and a halting hello.

When Mina had followed her into the house she saw that Mrs. Sipes had used a stick to draw patterns in the dirt floor as decoration. The little sod house was small, maybe a third larger than her tent. It would be snug and warm in the winter if they had a fire going but she thought the pile of firewood in the house and the pile she had seen outside the house was woefully small if her experience at Fort Abercrombie was any kind of guide.

The Sipes family furniture was quite spare except an elegant rocking chair set in a place of pride in the center of the room. There were two rolled up bedrolls along the wall opposite the space Mrs. Sipes had made into her kitchen.

Mrs. Sipes pressed a tin cup into her hand, it smelled of coffee. Though after four years around the army, the scent of it was incredibly weak.

"Thank you," Mina said as she took a sip. It tasted as weak as it smelled, and flavored strongly of chicory.

Freedom gave a shake of her rattle and smiled as she pointed at the elegant rocking chair. It was clear what she wanted.

"Would you like a sit?" Mrs. Sipes said with an awkward smile and a soft quiet voice. "I hate the thing but my husband and the girls love it. "

Up close Mrs. Sipes was younger than Mina had at first believed and prettier where she could see her clearly; hauntingly pretty. Enough so that she worried a little

47

bit what Johan might think of her looks. The reality was that Johan had seen many women far prettier than her and never once pursued any of them. He had looked and clearly appreciated, even spoken to them but he had never shown any real interest in any of them past being polite.

Mina let the young woman guide her to the chair. Freedom clearly liked the rocking motion and began to giggle. It was a comfortable chair. Maybe she could get Dale to build her one.

"Please call me Tisha," Mrs. Sipes said. When she spoke, there was a very slight halting lilt to her speech. Mina wasn't sure if it was an accent or not. She half thought perhaps this young woman was part or maybe even all Indian. Her face, eyes, color and radiant black hair cemented the idea. That both of her daughters had similar hair and color convinced her of it. By the apparent age of the two girls Tisha had to be older than Mina by a good bit but there was an ageless feel to the woman. She liked her.

"Your family is welcome at the bakery any time. If this winter is a cold one, I suspect we might be able to find room for you all on the coldest nights. I know Freedom and I wouldn't mind some company."

Johan ran his hands across the soft grass as he sat on the slope across the road and looked down at the property. The building with tavern and inn inside, the well house and stable were well set to take advantage of the crossing of the military road and the road north. A swallow of water from his army canteen felt good. It was good cold water from the spring that fed the well house. He looked with pride at the stone walls and foundations of the buildings. They really were quite the sight. Johan was surprised how much he remembered from constructing roads and buildings in the Legion. A wide smile crossed his face as he fully understood he was finally able to put that knowledge to good use.

Peter and his little brother were putting the final shingles in place on the inn. They were good boys in their own way. They were so young and more than a bit foolish. Had he or any other young men ever been all that different? Most that age only had women on their minds and these were no different. The way they looked at Mina when she wasn't looking annoyed him and the way they had stared at the Sipes women raised his ire. He understood they were just young men. But if they ever foolishly took it past just looking, he would have to deal with it.

Emmanuel and Willy were taking the last shingles up to the roof. Willy had been a good investment and Emmanuel a good partner. That Emmanuel had put forth a sizable bit of coin to buy into the place only helped.

But there had always been something a little off about Emmanuel, even before the war had changed him in such a brutal fashion. Without Nate he was cold and quiet and Johan half expected he would be that way the rest of his life. It had been a wise decision to build the room above the stable for him to live in. His nightmares were loud enough that putting the man in a room in the inn would have been an unpleasant mistake. Living in that room above the stable where his screams might spook the livestock was little better. Come winter sleeping there might be a challenge. Even with the small pot-bellied stove it would be difficult to keep the space warm.

Emmanuel was willing to work the tavern, which might just be a good thing and on the coldest nights could sleep by the bar. He had been pleasant enough with the veterans who had come through the place but more than a little standoffish with those who had never tasted the war.

Johan took another pull on his canteen and relished the cold water washing down his throat. The water was as good as any he had ever had before. Good water made memories and his memories of truly good water were few and far between. The water at the Barnaby place had been good but this was better. Maybe the best he had ever had. How no one had put a homestead on it he could not understand.

There were three established homesteads within two miles. The break in the rock where the water formed a thin steady spring that flowed down to the lake would have been ideal for a homestead. The small cave a little ways to the east in the side of the hill made an excellent root cellar. Maybe it was the lack of truly flat ground for farming within easy reach that kept anyone from claiming it... but even with that Johan really could not understand why no one had taken this spot with its excellent water and ready-made root cellar.

There were plenty of signs that men had camped here off and on for many years. As far as he could tell, the place never flooded. It was high enough and far enough away from the lake that there should be no worry of rising water. The ground was solid, if a bit rocky. Certainly too rocky to farm, but there were good enough open spaces only a few hundred yards away for fields or pasture. Hell, the Sipes had settled on one only five hundred yards down the road.

This place wasn't hidden, although the only reason he knew about it at all was they had stopped at the clearing during the return from an escort and long patrol. There had been a stack of recently cut timbers set under a rough lean-to left to season by someone. When the war ended, he had decided to see about homesteading next to the place or maybe even trying to buy it off whoever was there. When they arrived, they found the timber was still there and the lean-to falling in on itself. No one had any idea who had cut the wood; he figured they had likely died or fled, never to return, during the Dakota War.

Whoever had cut the timber knew how to use a broad axe, but no one had taken an adze to it. That lumber formed the heart of the stable and inn, and had saved them a lot of time building the place. He almost felt guilty for using it and half expected someone to come and lay claim to the property.

Johan grinned at the good fortune he had in coming across that plantation in South Carolina that garnered him the monies to build this place. It really was an amusing turn of luck. He had found a small fortune because Mina wanted a real bed for a night. So, he and his mess had gone to the abandoned plantation house to find one; only to find every bed, chair and table already taken. The place was even empty of internal doors. The only one left was the massive front door. They had taken it down to use as the base of a bed for Mina. Everyone had complained about the weight of the thing but had carried it to the camp anyway. It wasn't until the next morning when he was breaking up the door for firewood that he discovered why it was so heavy. Some enterprising soul had found a new and ingenious way to hide coin by drilling holes in the top of the door and dropping ten- and twenty-dollar gold pieces inside.

Too bad he had found it; a tragedy really. Some poor treasonous slaver deserved better. Well, at least they hadn't fired the house. Brick is hard to burn. That almost $5000 in gold coins combined with Mina's savings had made the inn possible. Emmanuel, deciding he wanted to buy into the business, only helped. Those monies had paid for almost everything to build the place and stock it as well as for a few sundries that he thought would come in handy. Emmanuel had his Spencer; Mina her Colt revolving shotgun and he had the same M1841 he had carried through most of the war. He had also picked up a couple other rifles on the cheap including a fine M1859 Sharps Rifle. If it ever came to it the place would be ably defended.

Johan knew he was lucky. He had money enough to drown in cognac. He had a few men he would willingly call friend. Most importantly he had Mina, a woman that loved him and that he loved back. If love was something he could truly ever give. He really had never felt love until whatever it was he felt for Mina. He was old enough to be her father, but she called him husband. He had never asked and was not about to, but he suspected she was only maybe into her mid-twenties now whereas he was... he was really not all that sure. He thought 1819 was about right which put him somewhere past forty and maybe even nearer to fifty.

Johan frowned at the thought of Little Miss Freedom. She was a bundle of joy that made Mina happy which was what mattered. He was always afraid he might break her if he played with her and was unsure how to react around her. She seemed to dislike him. Maybe that little child could see through to his soul to the monster that was there. She was no child of his but that did not matter; she made Mina happy and that was what was important. Emmanuel too adored the child, and her mere presence was a sure way to calm him and pull him from his darkest mood.

Mina read to the child every night and Johan listened as well, knowing that it furthered his education all the more. He was getting to the point where he could read mostly by himself, but some words still evaded him. Mina had said it would be time for him to start reading out loud as well. He hated to admit it, but that frightened him more than the idea of being on the receiving end of a bullet.

As Freedom grew older he and Mina would teach her French, and if she was willing he might teach her Dutch as well. He and Mina knew enough Lakota to get by; it would be a good idea to teach her that as well. He was fluent in three languages and could make himself understood in two more. Languages opened the mind and broadened the possibilities in life. The more she knew, the better prepared for life she would be. At worst she might take her knowledge of language to work as a translator and make some coin that way. All the fancy folk knew French, or at least pretended to.

If they could teach her to read and do the arithmetic that would be all the better. Education was the key to life; combine that with a bit of luck and a willingness to commit a touch of larceny…

How old had he been when he learned to pick a pocket? He remembered one of the women from the poor house giving him a beating for stealing from a passerby. He couldn't have been much older than nine or ten. That was about the same time he learned that bullies were nothing more than loud cowards and all it took to rout a bully was to smash him in the face with a brick.

Johan smiled as he pulled his pipe and tobacco from his coat pocket. He relished good tobacco and the stuff from these parts was not bad, though it was not the tobacco from North Carolina. That had been the finest he had ever laid his hands upon. Oh! What he would give for that North Carolina tobacco again.

He lit his pipe as the breeze picked up pulling him from his musings. Johan looked again at the construction across the road. They likely would finish in a few hours tomorrow. There was maybe another hour left in the day and Mina was preparing the dinner for them. That breeze brought him the hint of a scent from the coming meal. There would be more of her superb stew and sourdough bread. They were home, and for the first time in his life he was building something he could be proud of.

Hard Work Equals Good Business 1868

The Homestead Act, signed by President Lincoln in 1862, encouraged immigration like never before. By 1867 more than a million and a half acres of Minnesota had been settled. Wheat farming would become the main crop of the state by 1870.

Emmanuel cleaned the last glass and hung it in the rack above the bar. He turned to look at the rest of the glasses and couldn't help but marvel. Johan had purchased brandy snifters, wine glasses and a double batch of beer tankards. Only rarely were anything but the beer tankards dirtied. Yes, a score of bottles of fine liquor graced the bar, and there were the two or three men in the area who liked whiskey and wine, but beer was the favorite and few ever asked for Johan's cognac. The beer was made locally from two different sources, a brewer in town and a local farmer. One was a stout and the other an ale. Emmanuel couldn't tell the difference except by the color, and as far as he was concerned both were vile.

Mrs. Mina also made her contributions; there was a barrel each of dandelion and rhubarb wine as well as a basket full of her rolls every night. Only rarely did anyone draw a glass from those two barrels. Emmanuel admitted privately he was absolutely terrified of Johan's whiskey. He knew some of the ingredients and shivered at the thought of three plugs of tobacco, a dozen buffalo chips and a live rattlesnake... he really didn't want to know what else went into the poison Johan called whiskey. He would be damned if he would ever try it. But there were men who liked it; Emmanuel never had seen much that showed him men were overly intelligent. Life since enlistment in the army had done nothing to dissuade him of that idea.

The regular customers here were good people; he liked every one of them. There was the enormous Ivan, a man who had to be pushing seven feet tall. He would have made Sebastian look tiny. Emmanuel wasn't sure if he was Polish or Russian... not that it mattered, the man spent the best part of a dollar a night on beer, and he was there every night but Sunday. That he was also a veteran of a Wisconsin battery gave him a free drink every night. He eagerly made the two-mile round trip from his homestead every day to visit with fellow veterans and to enjoy his beer.

There was Vincent Kyle, who had lost his left arm on the first day of Gettysburg with the Iron Brigade. He was working on the telegraph line as an operator. He made the three mile hike every other day regardless of the weather to meet his friend Ivan. A truly good man who had lost much, but had made a life for himself anyway.

Emmanuel's favorite customer, though, wasn't a veteran. Korbel Mariner, a retired ox cart driver who had made a fortune on the Red River trail in the 1850's and more as a land speculator since, was a friendly and honest man. So, long as his money held, he intended to continue doing what he was doing. The man loved to come to the tavern just to talk to Johan and Mrs. Mina in French. Korbel called Johan his 'damned ugly Dutchman.' Apparently, there weren't as many people around that spoke French as there used to be.

Fall was coming and Emmanuel had a bad feeling that the winter would be another cold one. As a child he had learned that heavy snow and bitter cold were common in this part of the country. Emma had liked winter. It meant father would be away hauling wood into town more often. While he was away food might have been scarce, but it was worth it to avoid his temper and the beatings that came with it.

Emmanuel shivered at the memory of that winter in Ft. Abercrombie. It had been as cold as anyone had ever seen and Johan had insisted that they still work outside and drill even on the coldest of days. Most were used to winter but the extra time exposed to wind and weather had hardened and prepared them for the hard campaigning that came later.

He realized he was scrubbing a patch of the bar with a slightly darker stain. The piece was already clean but there was an uneasy feeling of trying to clean a bloodstained gunstock. It was bull but the thought remained. He moved to the window and looked outside at the tavern yard and the stable beside it. The first customers would be here soon. He glanced at the wood pile; there wasn't nearly enough. He and Johan had dragged deadfalls from a stand of trees a half mile closer to the lake. Between the two of them they had cut and split enough for most of the winter, or so they thought. They hadn't expected Mrs. Mina's oven to use as much wood baking bread as it had.

Johan had left for 'a month or three' on a job that paid fighting wages plus some. Things at the tavern were going well enough that Johan could leave with Mrs. Mina and Emmanuel in charge of the place with a vaguely clear conscience.

What the bastard had failed to take into account were the customers. Sure, the regulars were fine, but the influx of teamsters and loggers were another thing. Most seemed to be generally good me,n but there were always a few who were trouble. It didn't help that all but one of the boarders had left last week. The sole remaining boarder was a young tough who thought if *he'd* been in the army the war would have ended in a year instead of four… idiot.

Emmanuel studied the distorted image in the window. Emma's eyes looked back at him from Emmanuel's face.

He shivered as he realized just how empty and cold those eyes were.

A thump and a scream of anger from upstairs made Emmanuel's head whip around towards the stairs. Freedom began screaming in that piercing tone only an angry child could give. In this case it was the 'I am furious and will let the whole world know it' cry.

He grabbed the Spencer from behind the bar and ran out the front door to head for the bakery door. It would have been faster and more direct to take the stairs two at a time but the way they were built it was impossible to go up them without them squeaking loudly and alerting the wrong people that Mina had help at hand. Anyone who knew he was in the tavern would be waiting there for him to come up the stairs.

Emmanuel levered a round into the chamber and took the rise to the second floor and Mrs. Mina's bakery at a dead run. As he rounded the corner he saw Ivan, Korbel and Vincent walking down the road towards the bakery. They started at his sudden appearance with Spencer to hand. Then he heard the loud thunk of something large hitting flesh and Freedom abruptly stopped screaming. If anything had happened to that child the walls would be painted with blood!

Ripping open the door, Emmanuel stopped abruptly. Mrs. Mina stood in the middle of the room with her hair braid badly mussed, her headscarf was on the floor and a wide tear on the shoulder of her dress exposed more flesh than was decent. Her dark eyes were wide with anger framed by the tired circles around them; she was visibly tired but rage flowed off of her in waves. The long-handled steel frying pan she had used through most of the war was in her hand with a large fresh dent in it. Freedom sat on the floor calmly holding her precious turtle shell rattle in one hand and the small wooden hammer Willy had made her in the other. A man, the young boarder who thought he would have won the war single-handed, lay prostrate on the floor groaning while he tried to get his hands underneath him.

"What the hell?" Emmanuel asked from the door.

Mina looked at him from across the room. "Emmanuel, would you please haul this... person out the door? He is leaving." As she spoke she looked forlornly at the new dent in her fry pan and calmly set it down. She stepped behind the bakery counter and pulled her Colt revolving shotgun from its hiding place.

Emmanuel stepped the rest of the way into the bakery and grabbed the prostrate man by the collar and began to drag him out the door. He groaned and complained bitterly but was only able to feebly struggle. He stopped when Mina eared back the hammer on the shotgun.

"Let me up," the man slurred.

Dragging him the rest of the way out the door, Emmanuel propelled the man to the ground. He sprawled in the grass and rose to his hands and knees. Ivan and Vincent sprinted into the yard with Korbel puffing behind them.

Emmanuel stepped up behind the man and gave the man a perfect bayonet drill blow to the right kidney with the butt of the Spencer. The young fool crumpled to the ground a moaning ball of agony.

"Whoa!" Vincent exclaimed from fifteen feet away.

Mina chose that moment to step out of the bakery with that Colt shotgun in her arms.

Ivan abruptly bit off a curse from behind Vincent. "You ok, Mrs. Mina?" Ivan asked in his heavy accent.

The man on the ground groaned and rolled onto his back. Emmanuel jammed the muzzle of the Spencer into his mouth. There was the satisfying crunch of teeth breaking and a scream of pain which silenced as the hammer was pulled to full cock on the Spencer.

"Don't shoot him!" Mina barked.

Emmanuel took a deep breath in and eased the finger off the trigger, then let out a slow breath. A slow calculating look down at the man on the ground followed. The face was a mess, which was understandable after the insertion of a .56 caliber rifle barrel into his closed mouth. There was an enormous bump rapidly rising on the side of his head where Mrs. Mina had brained him.

"You're right, Mrs. Mina. Johan would hang him," Emmanuel said.

"Did he hurt you Mrs. Mina?" Ivan asked. His heavily accented voice was very low and quiet, frighteningly so. He had picked up a broken tree branch on the way to the bakery and held it now like a club. Vincent had fished a side knife from his belt and looked ready to start skinning the man.

Korbel chose that moment to arrive breathing heavily. He took one look at the scene in front of him and barked out a laugh.

"I see man has failed to pay!" He barked with a second laugh. But his laughter died, and he backed up a step, as Emmanuel and Ivan hit him with savage looks.

The man on the ground whimpered around the rifle barrel in his mouth. Emmanuel used it to push his head into the ground and he gagged.

"There will be no hanging here!" Mrs. Mina said angrily. "Stand him up."

Ivan stepped back from Mina and the shotgun. Vincent let out a low whistle when he saw Mrs. Mina.

Emmanuel used the barrel of the rifle to lift the man off the ground. The front site on the roof of his mouth was a very good persuader. The man awkwardly stood unable to stand straight due to the blow delivered to his kidney.

"I'll take him across the road, we'll bury him there." Emmanuel said. His calm was something of a shock, as absolute but controlled rage simmered just below the surface. He was ready to drench the earth with the blood of this bastard.

"There will be no killing here!" Mina demanded.

"Across the road is good," Ivan said with a frightening smile.

"No! No one dies today," Mina said firmly. "Turn him loose. He knows what he did, and he will never set foot in this place again."

Korbel stepped forward with his hat in hand and looked between Mrs. Mina and the man with the barrel of a rifle in his mouth. He shook his bald head in wonder. When he spoke, it was slowly and carefully.

"Son, you live now only because this fine lady insists upon it. If we were to walk you across the road and hang you, there is not a man inside of fifty miles that would think ill of us for it. Most would wish they were here to have helped after what you have tried to do.

"There is work to build the railroad. You may wish to seek employment there. If you show your face here again… well, young man, I know Emmanuel to be a fine shot. Ivan will rip your arms off or Vincent will carve you a new belly. And may God have mercy upon your soul if Mrs. Mina's Johan finds you." He shuddered. "He is a hard one; he will make sure you live three days before he allows you to meet his angel of death."

Mina carefully lowered the hammer to half cock and sighed. "Emmanuel, take that gun out of his mouth and go get his bag. I will not have anyone accuse me of being a thief."

Mina stood there the pure image of strength with her sleeve torn from her shoulder exposing her bare collar-bone and shoulder with that Colt revolving shotgun in her hands. One thing was certain; she would be no victim.

Little Miss Freedom stood in the doorway with an enormous grin on her little face. She was bouncing up and down on her bare feet enjoying the show in front of her. Her little hands wrapped tightly around her precious turtle rattle and her Freedom sized hammer sticking out of her pocket. Emmanuel asked himself: what had that little girl just learned?

Emma answered him. She had just learned that life isn't easy and violence is sometimes the best answer.

Mina ran her hands over the torn fabric of her blue dress on the table. She would have to make certain she repaired it before Johan came home. If he saw it and started asking questions Emmanuel would explain what had happened and Johan would probably go hunting. She did not want that on her conscience. Too many men had died for much less than what that little fool had tried to do to her.

Mina had no idea what she might have done had Emmanuel not crashed through the door the way he had. Would she have continued to hit the man with that frying pan until he stopped moving? She didn't know and was glad she didn't have a death upon her conscience and wondered how difficult it would have been to get that much blood off the floor.

All she had done was be nice to the fool. He had taken it wrong and thought she was flirting with him. When she realized her mistake, she had picked up Freedom as an excuse and thought he'd take the hint. He hadn't.

She had badly mistaken the character of the man. When he touched her she had panicked like never before. She hadn't been so frightened in years and she had fought back the only way she knew how. That frying pan was to hand, and she had used it. It cost her damage to a nice dress and a needed repair to that pan. But things considered, it was worth it.

Mina looked down at the table and at the two plates of sourdough rolls sitting there. She needed to take one downstairs to the tavern but she didn't want to see the questioning eyes of Emmanuel and the tavern's patrons. They would think they had saved her when the reality was they had saved that young fool. If it had been Johan instead of Emmanuel through the door, she would be trying to rationalize a death because of her. If it had just been Emmanuel it might have been the same but Emmanuel plus Korbel, Ivan, Vincent as well as Freedom? She could not face that.

Freedom squeaked at her from the floor and Mina looked down at her. She was standing there with the Bible trying to hold it up in her small hands. Mina felt tears forming in her eyes; she quickly wiped them away and took the Bible.

It was the Bible Seth had given her when they left the Barnaby place. She ran her hands across the softly shining brass cross on the cover and the beautiful metal latch on the side, then traced her and Johan's name that had been stamped into the bottom of the front cover. She smiled and knelt down next to Freedom. Freedom wrapped her arms around her neck and held on in a tight hug. Mina set the beautiful Bible on the table next to the rolls as she picked her up, spinning in a circle until she was dizzy. Freedom was laughing and so was she. Thank God for children.

"Thank you, Freedom." She said as she hugged her tight.

"Momma not sad!" Freedom said in her childish voice.

Mina smiled as wide as she could and spun once more around with Freedom in her arms. "No, no, my little Freedom. You make me happy every day."

"Bad man go away?" Freedom asked. Her brown eyes were so wide and innocent.

Mina smiled, "Yes, he will never come back."

Freedom pointed to the two plates of sourdough rolls and Mina laughed. Trust a child to make clear what was important. She reached over and handed Freedom a roll then set her on the floor.

"Momma has to take a plate downstairs; you can't eat them all." She smiled as Freedom took the roll handed to her and looked at it, then held out her empty hand for another. Mina handed her one and Freedom nodded as though that were the only appropriate action.

"Now you watch the door and say hello to anyone that comes through." Mina picked up a plate and opened the door down to the tavern. Freedom was busily munching on one of her rolls.

Mina took a deep breath. She was Mina Steele, the wife of Sergeant Johan Steele and a one third partner in the ownership of this place. She had no reason to be upset. Everything was going to be fine. She cleaned it; therefore, it was hers. This was her home and by God no one was going to dictate how she should feel except her.

As she opened the stairwell door down to the tavern she heard the voices from below. Vincent was speaking, telling the tale. "...and Mrs. Mina had that shotgun in hand. If that don't put the fear of God into a man nothing will."

Ivan spoke in his oddly accented voice. "I thought Emmanuel was to shoot him right there."

"No, no. Once Mrs. Mina said no, I couldn't. That isn't the first time that frying pan got dented on some man's head. She's one woman I will never cross!"

That wasn't true, she had only ever threatened with that pan and then she had been mostly joking. That was a good frying pan though. She'd had it since Charleston, and it had been everywhere she had been since.

Mina shut the door to the inn behind her and started down the stairs, letting the inevitable squeak of her steps announce her presence.

Willy had fashioned the stairs from one tree. He'd split the trunk, squared it on two sides and spit it in half then used the pieces from the squaring to make the steps. The stairwell was just eight feet high but not as steep as she had expected. She loved the look of them and the squeaking sound they made when someone used them would forever remind her that this was her home.

Johan stopped to rest beside the stream and to water the two pack horses. His second pair of boots were shot, the horses would need to be reshod again and he was just plain tired. He and O'Neil had covered the best part of six hundred miles in a little more than a month and a half of hard travel. They had eaten well off the land, taking antelope and deer, and he had been well paid for his time. He would be bringing five twenty-dollar gold pieces back to the inn plus two good horses he could sell.

He had done his job, and there had never even been the need to use his rifle in anger. In fact, there had only once been an uncomfortable encounter. They had twice seen signs of Indians, and that had been an old sign; he had no idea of the tribe. White men had been plentiful though. Scores of homesteads were popping up all along the trail south of Ft Abercrombie, and not all of those men were particularly honest. The man who had looked longingly at the pack horses had decided discretion was the better part of valor when Johan had asked him if he had any idea how long it might take to put a fire out if his legs were broken.

On the prairie a broken leg was a death sentence and a fire a taste of hell. They had encountered one prairie fire, and for the first time in his life Johan was happy to have been on the back of a horse. He had never liked horses but with the wind-whipped flames of fire roaring he was happy to plunge into the river horse and all and watch the blaze race past.

Johan took a few minutes to bathe in the stream. If he was right, he would be a long day's ride from home. 'Home.' He had never thought of a place as home before. It was a strange feeling. He was looking forward to Mina's cooking and a glass of his cognac. There would be work to do too. He hoped Emmanuel and Freedom would be happy to see him but in all honesty he kind of doubted it.

He was looking forward to standing behind the bar and handing drinks to his regulars. Men like Ivan and Vincent made the place feel like home. If a man enjoyed his job it was not work. He enjoyed serving men who had been on the sharp end of the spear; they were men who earned his respect simply by surviving.

Johan pulled himself from the cold water of the stream and looked to the two horses. While he had seen no sign of Indians or even of white men in the last two days he was still wary. He picketed the horses close to the pack saddles and supplies. Then he used his bedroll to create a false camp a few dozen paces away alongside the stream.

No man accustomed to the wilds would camp next to water. That led to uncomfortable encounters with nature. Bears and wolves needed to drink as well as men, after all. An encounter with a curious big buck or worse, a thirsty bear or wolf, was not high on his things to do.

He made a small Dakota fire hole and made a soup from the last of his jerked venison. It was good and went a long way to filling his stomach. He looked into his haversack at the last three hard crackers and a can of beans. He would heat the beans in the morning with the last of his coffee and work on the crackers the rest of the day. That would get him home. If not, then he would arrive hungry and tired instead of just tired.

Johan checked the load on his rifle and climbed the big cottonwood at the base of the hill. The crotch in the tree was only about eight feet up but it kept him off the ground and out of sight. He laid his back against the trunk and just watched. He took in the lay of the land, the clumps of brush and other trees along the stream bed. He had campaigned across North Africa, traded among the Lakota and Cheyenne lands, fought through the southland, and knew that a fool that failed to survey the land around him did not live long. All it might take was a shadow in the wrong place, a tree wider than it should have been, or a startled hare or bird, to warn a man his life was soon to become rather exciting.

The Indians he had encountered on the prairie preferred the shock of a quick rush and a fight that was over quickly. He knew he was an inviting target to any wandering warriors looking for revenge or even just an easy scalp. Though he had promised himself long ago that he would not go easily into the waiting arms of the Angel of Death.

Johan would never be able to say when he felt comfortable enough with his surroundings to sleep because when he felt the relaxation that comes with knowing one is alone he was asleep in minutes.

Johan snapped awake; unsure as to why at first. The moon was up and the sky was clear. From the sky he would have guessed it was at least an hour till dawn. Both of his horses were looking off to his left. He knew he was no longer alone though he heard nothing at first.

The sound of men talking quietly as they tried to move silently identified two dead men. These were not used to the prairie, or the hunting of men, so it did not take him long to pick them out from the trees. The smaller cottonwood twenty paces to his left had suddenly grown two men wider. He heard their whispered voices but was not close enough to hear what was said. The larger of the two shadows held a shotgun or rifle while the smaller held an axe.

Men with any kind of good intentions did not go prowling about in the night armed. They were staring at his false campsite and dead fire. The moon was bright enough that they could easily see the mound of his blanket. Johan saw no other shadows out of place and he waited until he heard one of the men pull back the hammer on his weapon. Johan pulled his own back at the same time. When they did not react, he figured they had not heard their deaths coming as his hammer clicked to full cock.

The man with the firearm raised it to his shoulder and leaned against the tree trunk for extra support. He did aim carefully, Johan would give him that. Then pulling the trigger, he put a hole squarely through a perfectly good saddle blanket. From the flash and report there was no doubt it was a rifle. Johan shot him. His shot went home about seven inches behind the flash from the percussion cap. The man never knew he had been killed; his visit with the Angel of Death would come as quite the surprise.

It took a moment for the other man to realize death was beside him. The man let out a curious yelp and turned towards Johan with his axe. Johan was already closing the breech of his Sharps rifle on a fresh paper cartridge and felt a grin cross his face as he fully appreciated the pellet primer which eliminated the need to fumble for a percussion cap. His second shot caught the axe wielding man in the chest and dropped him in his tracks.

Johan reloaded and listened carefully to the night. His two horses had reacted to the gunfire and were milling about, trying to get farther away from the dead rifleman and his dying partner. They settled and went back to their business after ten minutes or so of waiting.

A low moan came from the dying man, but Johan waited a further ten minutes. From his vantage he saw no evidence that would betray others in the darkness. He could see the bodies of both men under the light of the moon from his perch in the tree, and he waited patiently. The second man he had shot was curled into a ball, moaning pitifully. If there was anyone else out there, he wasn't moving. Johan just sat and waited. Those two had intended murder and he had no sympathy for their fate.

As the sun colored the east Johan silently slid from his perch in the tree. He moved in a wide circle around the stand of trees where the would-be murderers lay, seeing nothing except two saddled horses tied to a willow tree perhaps a hundred yards downstream.

When he was convinced there was no one else nearby he went back to the dead men. The light was enough that he could see them now as more than shapes. He stood there looking at the first man he had shot; that Sharp's bullet had torn the side of his head away.

The other was still breathing though Johan knew exactly where he had put that bullet and he knew the man would not live out the morning.

Johan looked down at that one. Blood soaked the ground around him. He used his boot toe to move the man onto his back and looked into the face of a dying man he did not know. Someone had given the man a solid beating. A massive bruise colored the side of his face and most of his front teeth were missing. No longer coherent, he had slipped into the delirium of pain. His life would last only a short while longer.

Johan walked to the dead man and went through his pockets, finding only a pocket knife and a silver dollar. A leather bag slung over his shoulder held a housewife, two unopened .58 caliber arsenal packs from the Augusta arsenal, and an Enfield musket tool. From the looks of it, Johan might guess the man had been about thirty. He had been clean shaven and fair haired, with hands roughend by the scars of a man long used to holding reins. A woman might have thought him handsome in life.

He walked to the second man he had shot and saw that he had stopped breathing. Blue eyes stared at the sky from a face similar to that of the other dead man, clearly a younger brother. Who had given him that beating? It had been a thorough one. He found three dollars in loose change in his pockets and a razor-sharp roach bellied knife in his belt. The axe was a good one but far from new. It had been heavily sharpened over the years and was of the type he expected to see on the continent instead of here. Both men were well fed and decently enough shod.

Johan walked to their horses. One was a gray gelding and the other an old brown mare that had seen better days. Both wore army saddles on army saddle blankets and the knots securing them to the nearby willow tree were intended to be easily shaken loose if need be. The saddle bag on the gelding held a curry comb, a large rasp file wrapped in an oily rag and a small jug of sweet smelling rum. The other held a spare set of socks that needed a good washing and a spare shirt. A badly battered army canteen hung from the saddle and another bag held an empty flour sack with an old sheepskin jacket and an almost new set of brogans. The roll behind the saddle was an old cavalry poncho wrapped around an army blanket. A worn army haversack was stuffed to the brim with dried apple slices. The mare had two old hand axes, a whet stone and a change of clothes in her saddlebags. The bedroll behind the saddle was a rough woven blanket with a cut in the center so it could be used as a poncho. A feedbag full of corn was slung from the saddle and an old tin canteen that looked like it would barely hold water pressed uncomfortably into the flank of the mare. Johan moved the old canteen to make life a touch more comfortable for her.

"Your men were certainly a mystery to me," Johan said to the mare in French as he stroked her nose. She nuzzled him as he ran his hands through her mane.

Knowing full well the saddles and horses might garner some extra coin he led the two horses back to his own. He picked up the rifle that had punched the hole through what had been a perfectly good saddle blanket, and studied it in the morning light. It was a Tower marked P56 that had seen hard use but been well taken care of. He doubted he could get more than $5 for it and keeping it was not a good idea. The P56 was not all that common a rifle. In fact, he had only seen two since the end of the war.

Johan pulled the shovel from his pack saddle and pulled the two dead men to the edge of a cut in the stream bed. It only took a half hour or so of work to tumble the bank down upon them enough that the coyotes would be unable to easily get at the bodies. He might have scalped them and mutilated the bodies to make it look like Indians did the work, but that was not his way. There was no need to put the blame of these on some innocent Indians. It was unlikely anyone would come across their grave anytime soon.

Johan made himself a breakfast of beans and coffee. It was good, but delayed his trip home longer than he would have liked. It didn't take long to set the pack saddles, after which he sat back down and finished his coffee as he went through the events of the morning. He just could not figure the why of it.

Well, it would not do to puzzle too long on it. Johan pulled the old sheepskin coat from the flour sack and set it across the saddle of the mare. He led the four horses into the water and went upstream a good mile before he found a large flat rock. He cut into the sheepskin coat and used a bit of twine to secure strips of it to the horse's hooves. That would obscure the hoof prints long enough to make his trail all but impossible to follow.

Johan turned north and headed home. The mystery of why those dead men had hunted him would likely never be answered. Though men murdering travelers was not unheard of or so uncommon as one might think. If they saw his fire and thought him easy prey, they had been sadly mistaken.

Thriving Business 1870

Hard work - endless days of it - could make a business. The lack of it would and often did destroy one. Money earned can make life easy. 1870 is the year of the Great Chicago Fire and the Franco Prussian War.

Emmanuel set the tankard of beer down in front of the little weasel named Danny and walked away before something was said that would make him want to throttle the little bastard even more than he already did. He was telling tall tales again, bragging about his heroics in the war. Emmanuel would have wagered a gold eagle the man had never worn the uniform. He half expected that if Ivan or Vincent heard Danny on the brag, the kid would find himself face down in the mud.

Danny kept talking about being at the big battle of Gettysburg and making the charge with the First Minnesota. If he was to be half believed, he had single-handedly saved the day. As far as Emmanuel knew, damned near every man who'd made that charge had been killed or wounded; all would carry the scars. Danny was too fresh-faced and too full of brag to be a veteran. Probably didn't even need to shave every day yet. Plus he spoke too lightly of death and sacrifice, all but making it a punch line of some sick joke.

What was it Johan said about his Angel of Death? If one treated death with contempt, that was the moment death noticed you? Emmanuel unconsciously shivered at the way Johan said it; it had always made him more than a bit nervous and it terrified Emma.

Where was Johan, anyway? He'd been back a month from his last purchasing trip to St. Paul and was tearing around the countryside doing Christ only knew what. He wanted Johan here when he threw the little weasel out. At least he hadn't fronted the little shite a drink for being a veteran. The three fresh faced young men hanging on his every word were little more than children; Emma wouldn't

76

have put any of them at much over fifteen. They were loud and rowdy but at least they were paying up front for their drinks.

"Well, hell, boys; the only real soldiers from Minnesota were out east with the Army of the Potomac. I know there were some Minnesota boys out west fighting the Indians to rescue the farmers from those damned prairie niggers." The little weasel had a voice that carried. Emmanuel squeezed hard on the beer tankard he was wiping down and looked down at it. His knuckles were bone white. He set the tankard down carefully so he wouldn't break it.

Emmanuel turned and looked at the braggart in the middle of his crowd. Then took a look around at the other customers in the bar. The place had about a dozen customers other than the stupid boys. All were regular customers but none were veterans except the brawny teamster from St Cloud; he'd been a teamster in the army as well. What was his name? Was it Brent? The man knew Vincent and they were friends.

"Say Brent, want a free beer?" Emmanuel asked quietly.

Brent perked up. The offer of a free beer was almost certain to get the attention of any man.

"Free beer? Emmanuel, why the hell couldn't you been born a beautiful woman? What you want me to do?" Brent grinned around his pipe stem as he spoke. His teeth were a yellowish brown from incessant coffee and tobacco use. The bushy black beard hid a face scarred by the pox. He'd gotten a bad case of lice last summer and shaved his whole head to get rid of the things and his hair was only really just grown back.

77

Emmanuel pulled his own pipe and tobacco from under the bar. Brent smoked a tobacco with some sage in it; it gave it a distinct scent that he liked. It might be a good idea to ask him where he got his supply from.

Vincent usually wouldn't come in tonight, but if he could be brought here, he'd show that little weasel Danny to be nothing more than a liar. He was only about a twenty- or thirty-minute walk from here. Say an hour there and back paid for with a couple beers; Emmanuel would be more than willing to spot them each another couple beers out of his own pocket.

"Go get Vincent for me, he should be in his rooms over by the telegraph office. Get him back here on the double quick with the promise of a beer and a show."

Brent knowingly looked at the little weasel and smiled. "Hell, yeah. Anything that will shut that little shit up. He was no more at Gettysburg than I was."

Emmanuel chuckled evilly. "I'd wager a dollar he was never even in the army." He paused a minute and smiled, "And I'll suspect nobody has ever even taken a shot at him."

Brent looked at him then with a slightly worried expression. "You wouldn't be thinking of introducing him to your Spencer, would ya?"

Emmanuel felt the grin fade from his face. "Might not be a bad idea at that."

Brent took his pipe from his mouth showing those badly yellowed teeth. "C'mon Emmanuel, you *know* that's a bad idea. The boy ain't nothing but a stay behinder. This ain't the war anymore, you can't just shoot any old son of a bitch."

The stairs squeaked, and Mrs. Mina appeared as if by magic to set another basket of her sourdough rolls on the edge of the bar. She smiled at the room and headed back up the stairs. Brent and the other regulars noted the rolls with appreciation. At least two men loudly thanked Mrs. Mina as she went up the stairs.

Emmanuel stiffened as he heard a low whistle from the other side of the bar. "Daaaaamn, there's some fine curves on that nigger! I'd drop a half dollar for a roll in the sheets with that!"

The crass comment was met with a shocked silence from most of the tavern regulars but the little weasel and his cronies failed to notice and laughed boisterously. From the way her back stiffened and her fist clenched there was no doubt Mrs. Mina heard the insult. But she didn't pause, choosing to ignore the insult instead of acknowledging it. She might have turned and ordered the little piece of horse dung out of the place, but she couldn't really. Not even here. She was from the old south and no black woman could have ordered a white man out of a place of business. But Emma might have, and Emmanuel certainly could.

"Hey barkeep, some more ale!" One of the cronies said as he motioned him to them.

Emmanuel remembered Emma and wondered how she might have reacted to such an ugly insult. Would she have gasped and run away? Or turned and taken her fists to the little weasel? Emmanuel closed his eyes for a moment and took a deep slow breath. Emma would have gone after the little bastard with her fists with no quarter expected or given.

"Brent, never you mind about Vincent." Emmanuel said quietly around the stem of his pipe.

"Oh hell... Emmanuel... don't you shoot that stupid boy." Brent said with a very worried look about his face.

Emmanuel noted two of the other regulars stand up from their table. Samuel and Frederich were brothers, big strapping farmers from just up the road to the north. Mrs. Mina had helped when their sister had almost died of fever last winter, and they greatly appreciated her bread. He looked at them and smiled wolfishly. They nodded their understanding. If they thought help was needed they would pitch in with more than a little enthusiasm.

Emmanuel smiled broadly at Brent and then almost sneered. "I wouldn't waste a bullet on such trash. I ain't never been rich enough to waste ammunition."

He set his pipe down as Brent just shook his head. Emmanuel walked up the bar to the disrespectful noise maker. He looked at him and his three friends.

"You know what, boys? I'd almost pay to see you try an' offer Mrs. Mina a half dollar to look under her skirts. I could make a pretty penny on betting whether she would brain you, or her husband kill you. I've put up with your brags about being in the war, but I will not tolerate you putting forth any kind of question of her virtue."

Two of the three younger boys laughed nervously as if to imply it was a joke instead of a mortal insult. The third set his tankard and some coins on the bar, clearly understanding it was time to leave. That one might be salvageable, understanding they had well and truly stepped over the line as his face reddened in shame and he started to apologize.

Only started. Emmanuel didn't give him a chance to finish. "Out. You boys are paid up. You can get out now. That kind of language about a good woman will not go on here. Get out and never you darken the door again."

The younger of the two boys looked surprised and the braggart blustered as the third follower turned to leave. Those two had likely expected a warning, instead they were being booted out.

Danny drained the last of the beer from his tankard. "Shit, you ain't gonna toss a veteran out over a comment about some pretty little nig."

Emmanuel felt his jaw tighten. "That woman you insult with every breath was with us through the whole war and earned the gratitude and respect of every soldier of the regiment."

He laughed loudly and spit sloppily on the floor. "A nig whore with the army? Who told you such tales?"

Emmanuel smiled carefully and took a deep breath, closing his eyes for a moment. He felt calm and ready to kill. That rage that bubbled just under the surface was growing and Emma wasn't telling him to calm down. "I was there and saw her from '61 till we mustered out. Which means she is entitled to a free drink for being a veteran with the Army because *she* actually was with the army. You," Emmanuel snorted in absolute contempt, "you wouldn't make a pimple on her ass."

Danny stood up abruptly. "Who the hell do you think you are and what does that even mean?" he demanded.

Both Sam and Frederich loomed over the braggart's friends and they took sudden notice; especially when every other man in the place had stood up as well and

Emmanuel would have sworn he heard the sound of a knife being pulled from a scabbard. Emmanuel knew full well all he had to do was say the word and these four boys would be pounded to a bloody pulp for what Danny had said about Mrs. Mina. The boy who had started to edge away stepped closer to his friends with a look of despair on his young face. *He* knew they were in the wrong, but he wasn't about to abandon his friends. Well, at least one of those fools had heart.

The look on that boy's face took Emmanuel back to the war for a moment. To the memory of innocence on Nate's face before their first battle. He closed his eyes and cleared his head with a deep breath and felt the old calm of a battle soon to come wash over him.

"It means exactly what I said. I'll add to it if that was too difficult for you to understand. You are no more a veteran than that stray black cat in the stable. What's more, I'd wager a double eagle you'd mess yourself if someone ever actually took a shot at you. Now haul your worthless carcass out of here."

"You son of a bitch! If you were half a man I'd ask you to come outside and we'd settle this like men!" His face was a pleasant shade of red.

Emmanuel smiled and almost purred. "Is that a challenge to a duel?"

"Hell yeah it is, you old woman," the little weasel barked.

Emmanuel pounced on the opportunity. "Fine; I accept. Rifles at fifty paces. Outside, right now," he said pleasantly and loud enough for the entire room to hear. "Would you like to appoint a second should you run off?"

The weasel blinked, "Rifles?"

82

"Would that be too complicated for you?" Emmanuel asked with a smile.

"I meant with fists." He spoke quieter now. Then shook in realization that his crowd was watching him. "I'm gonna pound you into soup!"

"Oh no. As the challenged, I choose the weapon. Rifles. If you don't have one, I'd accept shotguns at ten paces." Then smiled at the fear behind the boy's eyes. "Even a... boy like you can't miss at ten paces with a shotgun. You being a hero and all of the war. You wouldn't be afraid of a little powder smoke sent your way, now, would you?" Emma asked in the mocking sweet tone only a young woman could use.

"You son'a bitch! Why you ain't nothing but a woman..." He abruptly shut his mouth when Emmanuel lightly set the roach bellied knife under his chin.

Johan had given it to him on his return from the Falls. It was a razor-sharp blade with a fine bone handle that he liked. A thin line of blood started to work its way down his smooth throat.

"If something that goes boom is too much, I have a good knife I can lend you." Emmanuel all but purred and Emma fully approved. All he could see were eyes that were full of fear. Emma smiled as she realized what she was smelling; the braggart had pissed himself.

Emmanuel smirked. "If you need a few minutes to visit the privy first..."

The entire room was silent. Brent had set his big right hand on the shoulder of one of Danny's crowd. No one moved. The little scene playing out at the bar had the attention of everyone. All but a fool knew Danny was a hair's breadth from bleeding out on the floor.

Johan chose that moment to open the heavy iron bound oak door into the tavern. He stopped abruptly as he noted the silence and tension in the room.

Johan stood there a moment, a bag in his left hand and his rifle in his right. He set the bag down beside the door and took in the sight of Emmanuel behind the bar and the weasel standing with a knife at his throat. The man shook his head, and sighed loudly. "Emmanuel, to kill customers is bad for business. The dead do not spend freely."

He raised an eyebrow and wrinkled his nose in disgust when he noticed the puddle on the stone at the feet of the weasel. "Put down the knife Emmanuel." Johan spoke in a calm voice, but it was the voice of command Emmanuel knew well, and brooked no argument.

"If his wagon has need of fixing I am certain there are more than enough to do so properly here." Johan said while looking carefully at Danny.

Emmanuel lowered the knife and unconsciously wiped the small amount of blood on his pant leg then slid it back into the scabbard at his hip in a quick easy motion.

Danny's eyes filled with hate. "Good thing the old man came in or I'd have beaten you to a pulp."

He was trying to reclaim something lost from pissing himself.

Brent laughed loudly, too loudly. "Boy, that 'Old Man' just saved your life. I think you need to thank him on the way out the door."

Danny spun in place and glared at Brent. "This ain't none of your business, mule skinner!"

Brent smiled showing those ugly teeth. "Boy, I'd have a talk with your daddy about your language around good folk... if anyone knew who your daddy was, that is."

"Why you..." Danny started.

Emmanuel interrupted with a sneer. "Get in line Brent. Danny boy here challenged me to a duel and I accepted. Rifles at fifty paces or shotguns at ten. If that was too much I have a knife to lend the little..."

"Enough!" Johan barked; his voice snapping through the room like a shot. "I do not know what started this, but I end it now!"

Danny looked around, apparently still not realizing he was on very thin ice.

"This old woman insulted me, and I want satisfaction!" Danny said angrily. His face was beat red and his fists were ready to go to work. "I'm going to pound him to dust!"

Johan sighed audibly. "I fought beside Emmanuel; if Emmanuel is a woman, then that woman would still be twice the man you ever will be.

"Now get out and never again show your beardless face here unless you are in the uniform of a soldier and have come to apologize."

Danny looked about to protest and suddenly saw the rifle in Johan's hand. Emmanuel watched the realization spread across the little weasel's face. He was boxed in, had given a challenge to a duel that was accepted, and rifles at any range were not the way to grow old.

Johan saw the look on his face and smiled that terrifying grin of his. "Would you wish to borrow my rifle and step outside and face the rifle of Emmanuel? I tell you now, you will not survive such an experience."

Mina wrung out the wash rag and set it on the rack to dry. She was done with the work for the night. Freedom was in her bed and Mina was hoping not to be too far behind. Taking off her shoes and taking the weight off her aching feet was something she was really looking forward to tonight. That, and maybe reading a few passages from the Good Book to right her mood.

As she washed her hands in the basin Mina took a deep breath. The comments downstairs shouldn't have upset her so. Emmanuel had thrown out those who made them, yes, but that they had even made them bothered her to no end. She was a good, God-fearing woman, a good wife and a good mother. Shouldn't that be enough?

Johan and none that he worked or served with had ever dared call her such. He never allowed an insult to her, and she had no doubt men had paid dearly for doing so in the past.

But this was Minnesota, not the south. Slavery was dead and gone; at least she hoped it was. She knew there were those who despised her because of the color of her skin. She was a rarity here, a black woman. Percy and Clara Cooper had just moved up the road. The three of them were the only black people in the area so far as she knew.

The boy who made the comment... his father owned the only sawmill in the area and was a respected member of commerce. That the boy had been thrown out would create problems. She knew Emmanuel, and she had already heard that a duel had been mentioned. Emmanuel would gladly kill if given the choice. He was almost as eager to deliver death as Johan was.

Mina sighed deeply and rubbed her sore shoulder. All but two of the boarders were already upstairs either abed or soon to be. The other two were downstairs in the tavern. She snuffed out the two lamps in the kitchen and checked the single lamp burning on the Inn desk. She turned it down to a feeble glow and headed into her rooms.

Mina took off her head wrap and set it aside. She would need a new one before too long, perhaps she could have Johan pick her up some fabric in town on his next trip there. If she had thought about it she would have asked him to pick some up today.

She looked at the book on the table waiting for her. She was so tired... The Bible Seth had gifted them rested on her pillow, reminding her that reading some from the Good Book was never wasted. The letter from Carlie extolling the virtues of her two young children and asking when she and Freedom would visit was tucked in as a bookmark.

Mina smiled as she realized Freedom was snoring slightly and there was a second softer sound. She looked in to see the black cat from the barn pulled tight against her tiny chest looking up at Mina and purring madly. The cat had declared its allegiance.

That kitty had come so far. It had been Sebastian's pet, and then hers. Now it was Freedom's.

Freedom had worked hard today. Emmanuel had showed her how to use a club and froe to make kindling, and she had spent the best part of the morning adding to the kindling wood box. Then she had joined the Sipes girls to dust, clean, and do laundry. That was hard work for such a small child. Freedom was full of energy and always watching and learning. But she was tiny, too small for someone her age.

Mina worried that the child wasn't eating enough and not growing like she should have. Whenever she mentioned it Johan merely shrugged his shoulders and the Sipes girls both insisted she would grow up fast enough. They were right, there was nothing Mina could do to speed things up. Freedom would grow and mature at her own pace.

She looked down at her little girl. Johan had pulled the swing bed down and set it on the floor so it could be used as a bed instead of a crib. While Mina would have sworn Freedom was still tiny, she was growing so that she could stick her feet out of the bed if she wanted to and could climb out of it on her own.

The Sipes girls adored Freedom and never missed an opportunity to spoil her. While they were cash poor, they were rich in love and kindness. They loved to play with her and let her know that she was loved and adored as though she were part of the family.

Those two girls were growing into beautiful young women. Danielle and Sherrie were only twelve and thirteen, but they were already beautiful and would only grow more so as their bodies matured. Life had already matured them their minds and hearts past their years.

Mina was proud that she had been instrumental in their education. Sherrie in particular was a voracious reader. She was also a thinker. Mina would have liked to have known where she picked up that copy of Uncle Tom's Cabin. It had been quite unexpected when Sherrie had quietly asked her if that was what slavery was really like.

How to explain it to someone who had never even seen slavery? While Mina had never experienced the worst of slavery, she had seen it. She had been by the slave market often enough and been to plantations several times with the Missus. She had seen men whipped until their backs were ribbons and known of families ripped apart to pay debts. She herself had been bought as a child, so young that she barely remembered her own mother. But her mistress had been wealthy and benevolent as well as a strong-willed woman of the world. Mina had never truly suffered the worst. Thank God for that.

She started as she heard the stairs from the tavern make their inevitable squeak. Only the family was allowed to use those stairs. Though the Sipes women were permitted as well, they were not here tonight. So, it was either Johan or Emmanuel. And Emmanuel usually went to his room above the stable after he finished in the tavern. But it was too early for Johan.

She heard the door open and shut and watched Emmanuel walk into the kitchen. The light was low, casting shadows and the faint reflection of the lamp on the inn desk eerily reflected from his eyes.

She turned fully to face him as he walked towards her door. What did he want? He knew the rolls were done and that there would be no more until morning. All she wanted was to just go to her bed.

Emmanuel opened and shut his mouth several times in a wordless question. Then blushed quite hotly.

"What do you want, Emmanuel? I'm tired and the morning comes early." Mina said irritably. She was immediately sorry. Emmanuel didn't deserve such.

"May I look in on Miss Freedom for a minute?" He wrung his hands in a girlish fashion as he asked quietly.

Mina scowled at him and replied tiredly. "Wake her up, and you will deal with her." She stepped aside, letting him into her rooms.

Emmanuel stepped to the edge of Freedom's bed and looked down at her. He just stood there and stared. Mina watched his shoulders relax as he set his hands on the edge of the bed and just stared down at Freedom.

"She's so peaceful. Your own little bit of heaven." Emmanuel's voice was so quiet, almost girlish with wonder.

Mina moved to the bedside and picked up her Bible.

"Would you really have killed that boy tonight?" Mina asked.

"Yes." He answered simply.

"It's not the first time I've borne an insult like that." Mina said quietly.

"You shouldn't have to." Emmanuel said as he reached down and gently stroked Freedom's hair. Then shifted his hand to pet the cat behind the ears.

Had any other man alive touched Freedom such Mina would have brained them. But Emmanuel had known Freedom since she was a babe in arms. He had been the one who named her.

"I was only going to shoot him until he insulted you. Then the lying bastard was gonna get gut shot. He doesn't deserve a quick end." Emmanuel said with quiet fire in his voice.

Mina shook her head. "Do you really enjoy killing so much?"

"I don't know. I'm good at it."

Mina took in a deep breath. "You're a good person. You always have been and always will be. Don't let the hate destroy you."

Emmanuel stood up a little straighter and gripped the edge of the bed railing. The tense shoulders were back again, and he turned to look at Mina.

"God put you here for a reason Emmanuel. You were just looking at part of it. I'm another reason."

Confusion crossed his face. "What?"

Mina looked at the man like he was an idiot. "You brought Freedom to me, and you were one of those that fought to end slavery for my own freedom."

"One of thous…"

"Shut up," Mina said shortly. "Do you think Johan would trust any other man alive in my rooms? He sent you to look at Freedom to calm you. God put you here for a reason. It's up to you to discover that reason."

Freedom stirred. "Mamma?"

Mina shut her eyes and ground her teeth in irritation. All she wanted was to lay down and go to sleep.

Freedom stood up in her bed rubbing her eyes. She saw Emmanuel. "Fiddle?"

Emmanuel smiled. Mina put her hand on his shoulder. "Go get your fiddle; if she starts crying…"

Johan slid off the bar and ran a hand through his thinning hair. There was more gray than any other color now. He scratched his beard and figured that was the same. He stretched as wide as he could and cracked his knuckles before rolling up his bed roll. It was before dawn and he figured he was the first one up this morning. There was no sound from the kitchen above and he did not hear the telltale sound of a splitting maul at work on the wood pile.

He and Emmanuel had pulled down a dozen deadfalls from the nearby timber and spent some time cutting them into manageable pieces. Most still needed to be split but there was some good firewood there. It was nowhere near enough for the winter, but it was a good start. They would always keep warm, pulling in more if need be.

One of the mules in the barn started braying and talking loudly with the others. Trading those two horses for mules a couple years ago had been a good idea. Mules ate less, made less of a mess and took less care than horses. They had already paid for their weight in fodder around the place. And last night Brent had mentioned that he might buy two of them off of him before snow flew this fall.

The man had been well into his cups and likely had not meant it but the offer had been made. He might remember it, or he might not. Either way Johan did not mind.

Johan poured himself a glass of his cognac and sipped it as he stepped to the window. The sunrise had not yet sent the first rays of the day above the horizon and the moon provided enough light for him to take in the yard between the inn and the stable. He retrieved his pipe and packed it as he thought about last night.

Emmanuel would have killed that boy. That boy was the only son of Richard Grace. Grace was a good man, a pillar of the community, and Johan liked him. But had he lost his son there would have been hell to pay and then some. The man was not a forgiving soul and held a grudge, but he was also honest to a fault. Johan would have to walk over to the sawmill today and talk to the man. If his boy kept up the brag about being in the war, then others eventually would take exception. That his son was a known liar reflected badly on the entire Grace family and might cost him business.

He set the pipe aside and washed his face and hands in the basin. As the water rippled he wondered about Emmanuel. He had known the man for the best part of a decade and had never known the man had a sister until yesterday. Emmanuel had never spoken of it.

Kevin had written his letter on the back of a broadside advertising his gun shop. There had been an offer to sell him a new Ballard rifle but Kevin knew Johan would spend the money on the business. The broadside was pinned beside the door frame to interest anyone in need of high-quality firearms. The letter to him on the back need not be seen by anyone else.

Kevin had asked around after Emmanuel for Johan. Johan felt bad about asking him to do so, a man should be allowed to tell his own story and not have it pried into. But Johan needed to know. No, that was not true, he merely *wanted* to know.

93

Apparently, the father of Emmanuel had been a woodcutter who disappeared just before the war. Nate's family had been the nearest neighbors and they could not recall any details about Emmanuel. The family spoke only of a dirt-poor family without a mother. They knew of a quiet, shy girl named Emma who had gone to a few years of school with Nate. They thought she must have died just before the war. Such tragedy perhaps explained the disappearance of the father and how Emmanuel had come to the army. Kevin had written that the building — more of a shack than a cabin, only a little bigger than an officer's tent — was still standing, but was a poor homestead as it was not near any water. Which certainly explained why Emmanuel had never expressed an interest in going home and relished the room above the stable so much.

A dead sister and a father who had abandoned him... such was not as uncommon a story as one might think. The world was a hard place; it always had been and always would be.

Johan could think of few who had taken to killing as Emmanuel had. Before Nate's death at Allatoona Emmanuel had not been anything past a good soldier and a splendid fiddle player. Afterwards... how many had Emmanuel killed? He and Little Foot had been perfect copains. Comfortable in one another's silence when not on the hunt for rebels.

Little Foot was gone west in a fruitless effort to find his family. The odds were good that he was dead now. Even if he were not Johan did not expect to ever see him again. Emmanuel had mentioned several times that he should have went west with Little Foot but what would that have accomplished? Emmanuel certainly would not have been welcome in a Dakota or Lakota camp and the presence of

Little Foot with Emmanuel would have created problems in any white community.

Johan shook his head as he lit his pipe and opened the door to the first light of dawn. There was a strong red color in the sky and there had been a ring around the moon last night. Rain was coming. It would be a good day today no matter how things went with Mr. Grace. He reached into the rafters above the door and pulled down his M1841. The wood and steel of the rifle he knew so well felt good in his hands. Taking a deep pull on his pipe he started out the door. He needed to scout the timber for any deadfalls or strangers, and would swing by the Sipes homestead on the way home and see if that worthless husband Jeff had returned home or sent any monies to help the family.

As his legs took on their long accustomed stride he thought of those men who had fallen in the war. So many in the Legion across North Africa and the Crimea and too many in his regiment during what they were calling the 'War of the Rebellion' or Civil War. Johan preferred War of the Rebellion.

Many were just faces to him, he had stopped learning names lest he grow too fond of those lost. But try as he might, he could not help but learn the names of the men in his company. He had generally liked most of them.

It bothered him that there was no real marker over the trench where men had been lain to rest at Allatoona. There had been real worry that some local rebels would dig them up to desecrate them. Johan doubted that would have happened. The locals near the pass had mostly been loyal Unionists. He had known enough confederate soldiers to respect them and doubted such would have even crossed the mind of most of them. But a stone marker would have been best with the names of those fallen. A marker to remind the world a man had lived was a good thing. Even if the vines and grass quickly overgrew it, a stone would be there a very long time.

Should he ask Emmanuel where Emma was buried and if there was a stone there? Perhaps if a stone were set for the man's sister it might bring some peace? It had cost Emmanuel and the rest of the mess a small fortune to have Nate and Sebastian's bodies sent home after Allatoona but at least their families knew where they were buried. It brought them peace being able to visit their sons. Would a stone for a lost sister bring Emmanuel a measure of peace?

Lives Wasted, 1871

Time passes quickly when there is little more to do than work and live. Minnesota became the world leader in the production of flour in 1871, and the railroad began its inexorable trek westward, allowing speedy travel and freight transportation like never before.

Emmanuel set the axe down a second and wiped his brow. The sweat was a soaking one, and it felt good to work so hard. The sun was at its peak with a heat that the ground seemed to bounce back into you. Even with the shade of the barn and the nearness of the well house it was uncomfortably hot. The breeze made it bearable and it was far enough away from standing water that the mosquitoes and gnats were not too much of a chore.

The wood he had split today was pretty poor firewood. Cottonwood would burn — reluctantly, but it *would* burn — but didn't heat terribly well. Still, it was firewood of a kind and Johan was certain next winter would be a long hard one. Cutting poor wood that wouldn't heat well seemed a waste of time, but the work was tiring and looking at the stacked wood felt good.

Emmanuel looked at Johan working on his shave horse. He was shaping some rungs for a replacement ladder for the stable that had broken badly when a horse had kicked it. There were also several stall rails that would need to be replaced, courtesy of the same horse that decided they tasted good. The damage caused by that mangy creature hadn't been worth the coin the boarder had paid.

Johan wasn't really that skilled with tools, but he always gave it his best effort. Though it was only ever pretty by accident. Still, Emmanuel had to admit that as ugly as that work was, it worked and generally worked well.

In the last year Johan had helped two neighbors build barns and been instrumental in getting the church built down the road at the edge of town. The man really was skilled at working fieldstone; though Johan seemed to think when he did do a nice job it was more of an accident than skill. Emmanuel looked around the place. The barn, inn, stable, well house and even the outhouse were well built and would last.

Johan liked to help build, had said it left something of himself for the future. That was a good sentiment, but a load of hogwash. No one would remember Johan long after he was gone. Sure, there was the GAR, maybe even the Sipes women and a few neighbors. But the man had no family and few in their right mind actually liked him. Emmanuel had no idea how Mina had come to love the man or how...

Emmanuel snorted to himself. Who was he kidding? Himself? Emma? Was Emmanuel going to be remembered by anyone? There was no one, no family or loved ones, no friends, and there would never be a family or children.

Johan had tried to interest Emmanuel in Danielle, the older of the two Sipes sisters. But how to explain it could never work? Emmanuel could never marry; Emma would never permit it. Danielle was so pretty, prettier than Emma ever had been and so young. She had to be at least five years younger than Emmanuel.

Danielle was not really a flirt but Emmanuel was fairly certain the girl had liked him more than was safe. Thankfully, the oldest Moenning boy, Sam, had taken a real shine to her before things became awkward.

Emmanuel smiled as he realized that the younger of the two respective families had also taken a shine to each other. If all went well there might be a joint wedding in a year or two when Sam married Danielle and Fred wed Sherrie. It was clear both Johan and Mina approved of such. They made good pairings and their marriages would bring pretty children. The Sipes girls each had inherited the wonderfully dark eyes and lustrous black hair of their mother. More than likely the gift of the bard had come from their father.

Emmanuel had discovered the elder Sipes woman was an Indian, a member of the Fox tribe that her husband had bought as a child. Jeff Sipes wasn't a man he liked and Johan had soured to the man dramatically in the last few years. The Sipes man was a worthless wastrel that always seemed to have money but never spent it on his family.

All three of the Sipes women had suffered badly that first winter. If Johan hadn't stopped to check on them one day on his way back from town, Emmanuel was sure they would not have survived. Johan had insisted they come to the inn and move into the corner room at the top of the stairs. The three women had taken the best part of two weeks to get their color and full health back.

Neighbors had talked, and not talked well of it. Johan had helped those women, likely saved their lives but people who called themselves Christians gossiped and talked ill of it saying Johan was collecting women, turning the boarding house into something it wasn't, and worse, suggesting Mrs. Mina might not 'be any better than she should be.' If such talk ever reached Johan's ears, people would pay dearly for it. He would always be a violent man who wouldn't tolerate ill talk of Mrs. Mina, and he clearly liked and respected the Sipes women. If the wrong person spoke within earshot of Johan, people would suffer badly.

Emmanuel was rather proud of his own role in putting such talk to bed. He'd simply told the jackass who'd gossiped that no churchgoing folk had stepped up to the line to help three women, so instead they were speaking ill of those who had.

Anyone might have done it, but it was Johan who had taken it upon himself to check on them and force them to the inn. Had he not, Jeff Sipes might have returned a month later to a dead family.

The Sipes women had insisted on paying for their room and board by helping Mrs. Mina in the kitchen, laundry, and cleaning. In return, they had begun an education alongside Freedom. Between Emmanuel and Mrs. Mina all had learned to read and also to cook and bake for the boarders and the tavern. Emmanuel had taught them how to use a saw and a sledge for firewood and Johan had taught the two girls how to shoot as well as how to use a knife. That had surprised Emmanuel; he never knew of a man to teach a woman how to use a knife. Danielle was a splendid shot with a squirrel rifle and Sherrie was outright frightening with a knife in her hand. There was no doubt those two would be able to defend themselves should the need ever arise.

The Sipes mother was a mystery, almost always silent and watchful. Her eyes were sad and tired but her face looked young. She had to be near thirty but could have passed as a sister to her two girls. In fact Emmanuel was still partly suspicious that she wasn't really their mother. They had her hair and her eyes as well as a more than passing resemblance, and he would not have been surprised to learn all three were sisters.

Emmanuel went back to the mindless work of splitting wood. It was oddly calming and it passed the time. The tavern tonight would be full as the boarding house was full and the Moenning boys were likely to come and call on the Sipes girls. Mina would set them up in the dining room and be the good chaperone. Emmanuel might have liked to step upstairs so that Emma could observe.

His attention was caught by the axe head sticking into the wood. It took a bit of effort to free the axe from what he thought was a knot. On closer inspection a bit of rusted steel became apparent.

He pulled out his knife and worked the steel partly out of the wood. At first glance he thought it a ten penny nail, but it was too large.

Emmanuel motioned to Johan getting his attention. "Johan, come look at this."

Johan shambled over stretching his back as he walked. "What is that?"

"Don't know. Why I told you to look at it," Emmanuel answered.

With both of them using their pocket knives they freed the metal piece in short order. It wasn't very large.

"Broken picket pin?" Emmanuel suggested.

"No, too short and the back is mushroomed. It has been struck many times. I think it may be a stone chisel. But why is it in a tree?"

He looked at the pile of firewood. "It would have been at the base; almost looks like the tree grew around it."

Johan shrugged. "Looks to be of decent steel. You might see if the Smith will give you anything for it."

"You work stone, can't you use it?" Emmanuel asked.

"Too small for my work," Johan said as he walked back to his shave horse and the ladder repair.

Emmanuel looked down at the small bar of steel and wondered. That tree had been at least three hundred years old, if not more, before it fell. The more thought put to it the more it looked like the tree had taken root over it. If the tree had been anything other than a dead fall that had pulled up its roots when it fell, no one ever would have found it.

Mina looked out the window at Johan and Emmanuel as they worked. Johan was doing something on the shave horse and Emmanuel was splitting wood for the winter. He did so almost every day. Minnesota winters were long and hard. The wood fed the stoves for heat and for cooking and they used a lot of wood between the inn and the tavern.

It was hot outside, though nowhere near so hot as she remembered Charleston this time of year. With every window and door in the place open to let the breeze in it was not too bad inside, though she was glad Johan had built the bread oven outside. The oven lay on the slope between the inn and the well house built halfway into the hillside. Johan had talked of building a simple roof to shelter it and the steps up the hillside beside the inn from the rain and snow. But that would take a lot of wood and likely more work than it was worth.

A small noise behind her made her turn to see Freedom trying to lift a pot. It was almost too big for her and Mina moved to help but Freedom scowled and stubbornly lifted it up onto its appropriate shelf then eagerly turned to continue her chores. No one had asked her to, Freedom simply had. And she was always enthusiastic, if a little too quick with them sometimes. She already knew how to read and was pushing through books that should have been too hard for her to understand.

Mina gave her the same tasks she remembered having as a slave child. Stocking the wood box for the stove, dusting, helping with the dishes and putting them away when they were dry, as well as emptying the thunder jugs every morning. There were a host of other chores she did between the inn and the tavern. Mina didn't care for Freedom going into the tavern or stable but knew both Johan and Emmanuel appreciated her help there. She was only just six, but she was willing and always there wanting to help Emmanuel. She avoided Johan and never called him papa or father; he was just Johan to her.

Mina shook her head at that thought and watched Freedom putting away the dry dishes from the night before. Johan didn't know how to deal with Freedom. She wasn't his child, not truly. Though Mina didn't know how he would have reacted to one if it *were* his. Mina had wanted a child of her own but Freedom had met that want… at least she thought she did. She was an adorable and intelligent girl as well as a curious and precocious one. She had her opinions and let everyone know what they were, and Johan encouraged that. Freedom was no child to be seen and not heard. Most of the boarders liked her and enjoyed playing with her, even the hard men who gave Mina a bad feeling liked her. The growly old Italian teamster Mateao had even sat down and taught her how to whittle a whistle. He'd even gone so far as to give her a pocketknife of her own.

Freedom was growing into a lovely young girl and Mina suspected she would grow into a beautiful woman. She loved to read and to listen to people talk, especially if they were from a long way away. She often encouraged Mina to speak of Charleston and begged Johan to speak of Africa and the people who lived there. Mina liked to listen to those stories as well. Sherrie and Danielle would sometimes push Johan to speak of Europe and Africa when it came time to visit at the dinner table. Mina had a difficult time convincing the three girls it was rude to ask people of their past.

Mina knew she was going to have to talk to Johan about the Sipes women moving into the inn on a permanent basis. They paid their rent with real work around the place, and they were doing well enough that some wages could be paid to them.

She liked all three of them. Tisha was so quiet and watchful. Little escaped the woman's notice, though when she saw things amiss she rarely said anything, instead doing her best to correct them without so much as a word. Her oldest daughter, Danielle, was every bit as beautiful as her mother. Though somewhat taller and larger in build, she was still a petite one with curves that attracted the eyes of men.

There was no doubt Johan liked the child. He had taught her to shoot with a squirrel rifle he had found somewhere, and the girl was an exceptional shot. She brought in game almost every time she wandered the woods. Squirrel, raccoon and even once a pheasant; Mina could see the pride in Johan's eyes when he looked at her. At first Mina almost feared it might be lust, but it took no time at all to see that wasn't true.

Sherrie was the youngest of the three and perhaps the prettiest, though Mina was hard pressed to say why. Johan had taught her how to use a knife, which was something that bothered Mina. He had never tried to teach *her* the blade, or spent much time teaching her how to shoot well. But in his defense, she had never really asked and he hadn't offered to teach Tisha anything, which made her feel a little better. Johan had never once done anything to make her feel jealous. She had never seen him look at another woman the way he looked at her. When he looked at her he looked into her eyes and they never failed to soften, the hard edge would leave his face and his body would relax in a subtle fashion. She loved that reaction because she knew she was the reason for it.

Danielle chose that moment to walk in the door with her little sister right behind her... though if she did not know the girls she might question which was the older and maybe even if they were truly sisters. While they shared the same hair and eyes their faces were different. Sherrie hadn't yet grown into her face, but Danielle... Mina realized that Danielle moved differently than Sherrie. There was a catlike grace to her movements that Sherrie lacked.

Over the winter Johan had tried to pair Emmanuel with Danielle but while the two certainly looked good together they were not a good match. Emmanuel said Danielle was too young for him but there was something else there when he said it. Mina thought there was fear behind his eyes when he said that. Sam had taken a shine to her and Mina was convinced they were made for each other. Sam's little brother Fred had seen Sherrie from afar and had asked Johan if he might court her. That had been in the spring and Mina knew Johan approved of both matches.

Danielle pulled out a chair and sat down at the table, Sherrie followed suit. Sherrie pulled the ribbon that had been holding her hair in a loose ponytail and her hair spilled around her pretty face. She rubbed her right shoulder and sighed at the comfort that simple action gave.

"Mrs. Mina, do you think if Johan sees our father in St Paul next week he can make him come home?" Sherrie asked.

Mina blinked at that. Emmanuel had mentioned that Johan planned to travel to St Paul but hadn't known anyone else knew about it. "I don't know. I rather doubt it."

"Can you ask him to?" Sherrie asked.

"I suppose so. Your father loves you and will likely be back before snowfall this year."

Danielle sniffed. "No, he won't. He'll just find another excuse to stay in the city."

Sherrie blushed angrily. "Dani! Don't talk about..."

Freedom chose that moment to walk through the door to the inn with an armful of wood. Mina hadn't even realized she had left.

She dropped the wood into the box beside the stove and turned to study the three of them. "Why does Emmanuel bleed?" She asked.

Both Danielle and Sherrie were startled by the question and Mina stepped quickly to the window to look out at him splitting firewood. She hadn't heard him stop splitting wood... no, Emmanuel was still there, standing sturdily on both feet beside an ever-growing woodpile.

"What do you mean?" Mina asked.

"When I saw him this morning he was throwing a bloody rag into the outhouse," Freedom said as she wiped her hands on the little green apron Tisha had made for her.

"I suppose he must have cut himself," Mina answered.

"I saw him toss bloody rags in the fire last winter."Sherrie said. "He said it was an old wound that bleeds once in a while."

Mina scowled slightly. She knew he had been wounded during the war but not that the wound still troubled him. If that was true it might explain some of his irritability. Long term pain… but she had never known. Was he that good at hiding it?

"It's possible. I know he was wounded but I didn't know it still pained him," Mina said.

Danielle raised a dark eyebrow. "I saw him burning bloody rags too. Though that was last year before snowfall. He said he had cut himself in the leg."

Mina considered that. Maybe he was cutting himself. She would have to ask Johan to talk to him about it. She moved back to the table.

"So, ladies, we were going to work on our French during the heat of the afternoon." Mina said as she pushed the three slates and chalk towards the girls.

"Mama, what does 'copain' mean?" Freedom asked.

Mina felt herself smile. "It means friend or companion. The feminine would be 'copine.'"

"Emmanuel, he cries sometimes in the night." Freedom said.

Both Danielle and Sherrie looked at Freedom with puzzled looks and Mina narrowed her eyes.

"When have you seen him cry at night?" Mina demanded.

Johan set down his parcel and rooted through his pocket for the coins Emmanuel had given him to purchase cartridges for his Spencer rifle. He found his tobacco instead. That wasn't a bad idea, so he filled the bowl and lit it, enjoying the feeling of calm that washed over him. As he smoked he pulled out the coins and just stared at them. A pair of ten-dollar gold eagles. They had been heavily used and were far from new even though both were minted in 1864. The face had been almost completely worn off of one and the other bore teeth marks from someone testing the gold content at least once.

Emmanuel had wanted him to pick up a case of cartridges and a replacement magazine tube for his Spencer with the supplies. How long would it take him to go through a thousand cartridges?

Johan let out a cloud of tobacco smoke and looked to the sky. It was clear with only a few clouds breaking up the afternoon sky. He could smell horse manure and fresh bread being baked as well as hear his mule stomping in the little alley to his left. The wagon was full and the crate of cartridges would have been the last thing in the cart. Everything else was to be delivered in a few weeks.

He had bought a couple of nice sundries for Mina. Hairpins, a beautiful ivory comb, a new mirror and some very fine knives for the kitchen as well as more books that he hoped the girls might enjoy. With the liquor, coffee and such the wagon was full. Would the things in the wagon be appreciated? Did it matter?

He closed his eyes and looked at the two coins in his hand and considered. Men had killed for such coins in the past; men had killed for considerably less. A man was likely to die now because of those coins. If he hadn't stopped at this store for those Spencer cartridges...

Outside the gun shop he had encountered a noticeably pregnant little Irish woman named Cara. She couldn't have been much over sixteen. She had asked him for directions to the Catholic Church and he had gladly given them. He had stepped into the entry of the gun store as Jeff Sipes emerged from the land office next door. Sipes hadn't seen him but the woman had, and she gleefully threw her arms around his neck calling him husband.

Johan simply stood there in the shadows watching. It was apparent that the man he knew as Jeff Sipes was also known to this young woman, his wife, as Jeffery Piper.

Johan could feel the rage rise in him; he wanted nothing more than to feel that thick throat under his hands and to watch the life leave those blue eyes. He had not felt such rage in a long time.

The man had a wife and two wonderful daughters. His wife was beautiful and loyal. The man did not deserve those women and from what he could see of the young Irish woman carrying his child he did not deserve her either.

Johan stood there and pondered the question of what to do about it. Sipes was a poor provider for his family across the road from the inn and it was unlikely he would do better for this pregnant one. No woman alone with an infant would have it easy here, or anywhere else.

For a half second he imagined the sound and feel of a blade sinking home into Sipes stomach. He only came to his senses when he realized he was caressing the bone handle of the blade at his hip. Such a thing could not happen here.

Before the war he might have been able to do so, but now? Now there were too many who would want the law to find a culprit. Too many of the gentry had moved in. When the lawyers and gentlemen arrive to civilize a land, the place always took a turn to the corrupt.

If he knew when the man might next head north, that would be the time. A bullet from the tree line, a missing scalp and mutilated body to lay the blame on the Dakota. But such a thing was wrong, grossly wrong. The Indian had been on the short end of the stick for too long as it was. Johan would not be one to make it worse.

Johan watched the back of Sipes and his newest wife disappear down the street. They were passing a new school still being built. The rapidly rising school gave him an idea.

A school was needed at home. The Sipes homestead would make a good school site. It was only a few hundred yards west of the crossroads and well suited for the children of the area. A real school building might be a good addition to the area. The house was too poorly built to be useful, but the barn the small horse barn might be converted into a school without too much trouble. A reasonable price for that land could be raised and might set those women for a while; long enough to recover from the loss of the likes of Jeff Sipes.

Chances Taken
Spring 1872

A community is built with churches, schools and business around a cross-roads or group of people. The Metropolitan Museum of Art opens in New York City and suffragette Susan B. Anthony votes for the first time, receiving a $100 fine for doing so.

Emmanuel crossed the tavern to meet Johan as he emerged from the passage behind the stairs. Johan took the crate of pickle jars Mrs. Mina had sent down and grunted as he turned and went back into the cellar behind the stairs. The overhang had been there long before the place had been built, and judging from the soot-blackened ceiling it had been used as a campsite many a time. Walling it up and using it as cold storage for the tavern and inn only made sense. Digging a passage through the hill into the well house had been a brilliant idea. Now one could move between the inn and the stable without feeling the sting of the winter wind or being seen if need be. As only a very few people knew about that passage, it was also a good place to disappear should one need to. Freedom liked to disappear into the tunnel with a candle and read when she wanted to be alone.

Johan may not ever have received a real education, but the man was sly and more than a little wise in the ways of people. Mrs. Mina and Seth had spent the better part of three years teaching the man his letters and they had done a good job. He was a changed man from the brutal soldier Emmanuel had first seen on the parade ground of Fort Snelling. He had softened some, no longer so quick to violence and most of all he only rarely cursed anymore.

He had to admit he was jealous of the man and Mrs. Mina. There was real love between the two of them. But what was love, really? With those two it was an unbridled affection, respect and appreciation for one another. They also complemented each other; Mrs. Mina calmed Johan like nothing else Emmanuel had ever seen. And Johan protected Mrs. Mina. It was easy to forget that she was a black woman around Johan. The term nigger never once crossed his lips and may God have mercy upon any who insulted her, for Johan would not. That was what both Emmanuel and Emma were jealous over. That kind of relationship was not an option for Emmanuel.

There could never be love or appreciation like that between Emmanuel and anyone else. Neither Emmanuel nor Emma had ever been exposed to anything like it, never experienced it. There was no memory of mother, and father... Father had tried, but he was not cut out to be a father. He had done what he could to feed, clothe and see Emma got some kind of education. To be honest, that really was a lot.

Emmanuel went back to the duties of the tavern. Glasses had to be polished, there were still some that needed washing. The bar could use a coat of oil and the brass pole along the bottom needed a polishing. There was a never-ending parade of things that had to be done. It was enough to keep Emmanuel busy, but it was the kind of work that let one think. Once in a while thinking too much could bite you.

Johan was helping to build. He had helped build a church, two barns, a house and was now talking around the neighbors that a school would be a good idea. People would come to him for advice. He was a respected man of the community. While Emmanuel was... just the growly bartender who worked for Johan.

What was there worth remembering about Emmanuel? Who would call Emmanuel friend? Mina, Johan, Freedom? Maybe Ivan, Vincent and the Sipes women? When it came time to be set in the ground, who would mourn?

A tap of inquiry on the heavy wooden door to the tavern brought Emmanuel from the dark thoughts beginning to cloud the mind. "We aren't open yet, but you can come in; coffee's on if you like."

The door swung open slowly and the sheep bells Johan had bought from a tinker in the summer played their chime. An old Indian strode in and looked up at the sheep bells. He had probably been tall and strong in his youth but now he was stooped with age and looked haggard, his hair as white as the winter snow. A crooked smile crossed his proud face.

"The woman above said to look here for the French warrior." His English was slow but careful; he took some time to consider his words before he spoke.

There was a large knife in his belt, and he held a stout stick with a bit of antler lashed to it as a walking stick. An old, battered army canteen hung slung over his shoulder and worn moccasins with a buckskin shirt dirty and worn thin in places underneath a ragged cavalry shell jacket were mute testimony to long miles behind him.

Johan chose that moment to emerge from behind the stairs. He stopped a moment and stared. Then he spoke in a tongue Emmanuel didn't know. It sounded like Dakota, but different enough that it was difficult for Emmanuel to sort out, not that he was fluent in the language to start with. The two conversed in this language for several minutes.

The old Indian walked up to the bar, close up he looked much like Little Foot. He had the same distinctive features, the same shape to his eyes but the man had to be in his seventies or eighties.

"To open trade." The Indian said with a grin as he placed a small nicely made patch knife on the bar.

Johan laughed, "You need not pay my friend. I will ask my Mina to make up a room for you."

The old man scowled. "I have never slept in the white man's bed. I will not start now."

He drew the large knife from his belt and set it on the bar next to the patch knife. It had been sharpened so many times there was a wicked looking curve to the blade that likely had not been there when new.

"Good food and water is what I ask. I will sleep where I was born."

Emmanuel scowled in confusion then decided perhaps the man would appreciate a beer. As he moved to fill a tankard Johan touched him on the arm and shook his head no.

"Would you part with some of your lemonade?" Johan asked quietly.

Emmanuel looked at the old man who was looking around the inside of the tavern with some interest. "Sure."

"Thanks, no liquor for this man." Johan said quietly.

Johan thanking him? That was fairly rare. It was nice though. Who was this old Indian to Johan?

"How do you know Johan?" Emmanuel asked as he set a tankard full of the precious lemonade before the Indian.

He looked at Emmanuel a long moment before answering.

"You are a warrior." It was not a question.

"Yes, I fought with Johan in the War." Emmanuel said.

"There is much sorrow in your eyes. You are the friend of Little Foot."

Emmanuel felt his eyebrows shoot up and mouth drop open. But it was Emma who exclaimed: "You know Little Foot!"

His eyes were very sad but he chuckled softly. "He lived among my people. He sent the horse I bring to you."

Johan put his rough hand on Emmanuel's shoulder. "Little Foot is gone."

Emmanuel started at his touch. "What?"

"Spotted Owl has come to tell us he is gone." Johan said.

"G-gone?" Emma asked but Emmanuel knew. Their best friend was dead.

Mina looked out the window to the yard. Most of the snow was gone now, only small patches on the north slopes remained. Winter was all but gone. Enough so that the Sipes women had moved back to their house last week, just in time for Jeff Sipes to return. He'd been gone all winter, not even bothering to return for Christmas. She had really come to dislike the man. Tisha and her girls deserved better. He hadn't even bothered to send money home!

If the girls hadn't been in the inn with her over the winter they might well have starved. They would certainly have frozen. She moved to the stove and added a piece of firewood to keep the oven heat steady. Then moved to look south toward the lake again.

The old Indian walking in the door had been a pleasant-surprise. He had looked familiar, but it had taken her a minute to remember him. When Johan had been trading with the Indians they had stayed at his village for several days, a place they called Cherry Creek. It had been as far west as they had gone. It was a barren country of long grass, but she had liked the women there. The last dozen years had aged the man badly. When he had asked for the "French Warrior" she knew instantly he was speaking of Johan. She didn't have any idea why but she wanted to hug him.

She watched Spotted Owl and Johan walk to the stable. Emmanuel was just sitting on the shaving horse looking south. Smoke curled from the pipe in his mouth. He did not move even as the wind twisted his old army greatcoat in what had to be an uncomfortable way.

Johan and the old Indian led a horse from the water trough beside the barn and Mina started. That looked like the roan Little Foot had bought just after the war. It was older and stronger. Little Foot had doted on that horse. He would never have parted with it, so where was he? It took a moment for the reality to dawn on her, and she covered a gasp with a hand to her mouth. The man had come a long way to get here. She considered that distance; that had to be the best part of a two-month journey by wagon. By horse, maybe half that. It was a long way, only an important task would bring a man that far.

Little Foot was dead, that was the only reason she could imagine that would bring an Indian this far to the east. Little Foot had become the only real friend of Emmanuel. Johan had called them 'copain' or friend. But friend didn't really define that French word. They had acted more as
119

brothers. Both had lost everything. Emmanuel had lost Nate, and Little Foot his people... others might have said Little Foot lost more but Mina knew Emmanuel had completely fallen apart with the death of Nate.

"Mama, who's that?" Freedom asked from beside her.

Mina started, she hadn't even realized Freedom was in the room. She looked down at the precious child and smiled. She didn't know why but she felt tears begin to swell in her eyes.

"Freedom, can you help me?"

"Yes," was her simple answer.

Mina felt herself smile. This child was truly a gift from God. The good Lord could not have sent a better one to her.

"Go to Emmanuel, stay with him. He is in great pain and you can help him just by being near him."

Freedom looked at her curiously, her dark eyes soft in the light. "Can I bring him his fiddle?" she asked hopefully.

Mina smiled. "That might be a good idea, though don't be hurt if he doesn't want to play."

Freedom hugged her leg and ran out the door. A few moments later she watched her run down the hillside beside the stairs and disappear into the stable. She knew right where Emmanuel kept that fiddle. She chuckled and remembered when Freedom had hidden the fiddle in an effort to tease Emmanuel. The man hadn't noticed and Freedom had fumed for three days before she got angry and took it to him with a demand that he play.

As she emerged from the stable with the fiddle Mina watched Johan gesture to Freedom with a smile. That wasn't something Johan often did. The old man watched Freedom trot across the yard to Emmanuel. Mina wasn't close enough to hear what was said through the window but she could imagine the demand for him to play. It took a minute for him to look at her and he shook his head no. So, Freedom simply crawled into his lap. Emmanuel looked surprised for a minute then softened and held her; his face disappearing into the top of her head.

Mina turned away from the window and felt a wash of tears slide down her cheeks. She had never been close to Little Foot. She had only rarely spoken to the man; but he was one of the men she might have called hers. A man she respected, and she knew Johan had liked him. His death should not have made her feel this way. It was a fact of life that men died; but he was one of hers and he had lived through the war, only to die now.

Johan walked through the woods just looking at the trees. Spotted Owl had described an enormous old willow tree. It should not have taken so long to find, as his directions had been quite good. He was about to give up, thinking it had fallen, when he found it. It was as described but a wind sometime in the past had broken a large part of it away and it was shorter than he expected.

He began to clear brush and dead limbs away from the base and discovered the circle of heavy rocks Spotted Owl had spoken of. From that discovery he was able to find the place that had been described to him. It had been a good spot to winter. Water nearby in the creek with ample trees and the hill to break the wind. Game would have been plentiful with birds at the lake and deer in the woods. The heavy thicket to the north would have made it difficult to approach from that direction and the swampy ground to the east would have done the same. The heavy woods to the west had been greatly cleared of timber in the last few years and would have been the direction a threat would have emerged from.

It did not take Johan long to find and fell four fairly straight pines. It took considerably longer to trim them. By early afternoon he had completed the structure as described to him. He hoped it would work as intended.

It was nearing midafternoon when he stepped onto the road to the west of the Sipes place. He was tired and looking forward to a hot cup of coffee in the tavern. The rifle slung across his back was a reassuring presence and the axe in his hand felt good. It had been a day of hard but good work. He was doing the right thing. Perhaps that would count some when it came time to be judged. The Angel of Death came for everyone when it was time. Nothing could stop her, nothing should. Maybe she would be more likely to smile if a man had led a decent life.

His thoughts were interrupted as he saw Tisha emerge from the trees to the south of the road. She struggled under a heavy bundle of firewood. Johan felt his brows furrow. He knew Jeff had returned. She should not have been the one gathering firewood. That thought made him realize he had been hearing the rhythmic rise and fall of an axe chopping wood from the time he had stepped from the woods.

Tisha stopped beside the road to shift the load to a more comfortable position and Johan could see the heavy sweat on her face and the strain there as well.

Where was Jeff, and why was he not doing this labor? He changed his direction slightly and moved to meet Tisha as she crossed the road. She had not seen him and when he spoke Tisha nearly dropped her bundle in surprise.

When she spun to face him her face was flushed and for a moment there was fear behind her eyes. That fear was replaced by embarrassment and she cast her eyes down to avoid his eyes.

"Jeff is home I see. Where is he now?" Johan asked. It was difficult to keep the anger from his voice.

"He went to town this morning." She said quietly. She was always so soft spoken. When the woman smiled, which was rare, her whole face lit up and she became truly beautiful. Maybe that was what angered him so much about Jeff Sipes.

Johan looked at her and shook his head. "He should be doing this work, not you. Hand me your bundle and I will carry it to your daughters for you."

She shook her head. "No, he will be angry if he sees you."

Johan felt his lip curl and he smiled, noting the expression of fear on her face. "I will speak to him. That is something long overdue."

He reached and took the heavy bundle from her. She shied away as Johan shifted the axe to a more comfortable position so he could more easily carry the load. She was not quick enough to cover the bruise on the back of her neck. Johan ground his teeth in anger. He was going to look forward to that talk with the bastard.

"Do you know how much your husband paid for the homestead?" Johan asked through clenched teeth.

"He never speaks of money to me," she answered quietly.

"I will speak to him of it. A school is needed. Your barn would make a good one."

She stopped and looked at him with a confused expression. "I do not understand."

"You will receive $200 in gold coin for the land." The ground underfoot was soft and Johan had to be careful to not stumble.

Tisha moved beside him. "He will not accept."

Johan smiled again as Danielle and Sherrie came into his view beside the sod house. "He will."

"He will want more money. Where will my daughters and I live?" She asked with some irritation in her voice.

Johan did not pause for thought before answering. "You will move into the room at the top of the stairs. Mina adores the three of you and Freedom calls the three of you her family. Your family will be welcome."

"He will never accept; there is not enough room for him in that room with us."

"I know," Johan replied simply.

Tisha did not reply but simply walked behind him. Neither Danielle nor Sherrie acknowledged him when he set the bundle of firewood down beside their woodpile. He buried his axe in the stump that had been used as the base to split wood.

Johan went cold when he saw the bruise over Sherrie's left eye. He stepped towards her, and she quickly nodded her head and looked towards the sod house.

Johan turned his head towards the house as he heard the door open.

"Brought them another axe, good," Jeff Sipes said cheerfully as he emerged from the darkened doorway.

Johan looked at him a moment then turned to Tisha and her girls. "Mrs. Mina needs help this afternoon. There are three new boarders due at the inn tonight." It was everything Johan could do to remain calm.

A dark look crossed Sipes face. "Go ahead, I'll finish the wood pile and feed the horses."

Tisha dashed into her house and grabbed a shawl. Then gathered her two daughters and rushed across the yard towards the inn. Johan pulled the axe that the Sipes girls owned from the stump and handed it to Jeff. Then pulled his own loose.

He looked at the blade and took a deep breath. "This is mine. I used it to set a scaffold for a man to rest today." The dead eyes of Spotted Owl came to his mind as he spoke.

"A ditch is more than any prairie nig..." Johan did not give him a chance to say more as he buried the handle of his axe in the man's stomach.

The doe foot of the handle connected nicely just under the sternum and Sipes collapsed in surprise. Johan set the blade of the axe just under the prone man's left eye. Johan knew the blade was sharp, maybe too sharp as it split the skin there. Or perhaps he used a little too much force.

"Did you come home to watch your women work and steal their horses, or just to see if they survived the winter?" Johan hissed between his teeth.

Sipes gasped for breath and looked fearfully at the axe blade resting on his cheek. He started to raise his hands to ward off the blade but Johan stepped on the man's hand eliciting a gasp of pain.

"You will take your horses and be gone from this place by the morrow. If I ever put my eyes upon you again it will be to bury you," Johan growled. He could feel the rage building, hate coursing through him. This man was a hair's breadth from death and both of them knew it.

"You live now only because I do not know how your other wife and child would fare without you."

Real fear was present in Sipes' eyes, and he started blinking his left eye frantically as a trickle of blood entered it. "I saw those bruises on your women. For that you don't deserve to live." Johan snarled then spit on the man. "You live now only because of your women. I want you to understand that. If they return in the morning and you are still here…" Johan let the words trail off in a silent threat. He trusted he had made his point.

Johan raised the axe from the man's face and watched the hate and fury rise in the eyes of Jeff Sipes. Those eyes were filled with malice. He had just given the man a target to aim at, but why make it easy for him? Johan brought down the hammer of the axe on the prone man's right collar bone and smiled slightly as he heard the snap of a broken bone and the ensuing cry of pain.

"Do not test me by letting me find you here on the morrow. I will bury you where you fall," Johan said quietly.

Cold Pain
Winter 1873

The winters of the early 1870's remain among the longest and most severe on record. 1874 had more than 170 days with temperatures below 50 degrees. The record still holds today.

Emmanuel turned as the door to the tavern opened with its distinctive ring from the sheep bells. Two men in heavy coats entered, along with a gust of cold air that brought snow with it. The younger of the two was one Emmanuel recognized; although it took a moment to realize from where. Johan had tossed the young man out on his ear when he tried to start a fight with Korbel. He'd also kept the knife that had been in the young man's boot.

The other man was taller, with a lean runner's build a vicious wide scar ran parallel to the brim of his wide brimmed hat. His mustache and beard were carefully trimmed, and he was well dressed in store-bought clothing. The taller man shivered noticeably as both moved to the stove and rubbed their hands in an effort to warm them. When he had brought some warmth into them, he opened his coat and Emmanuel saw the pistol at his hip. He pulled a tobacco pouch from a pocket, but instead of loading a pipe, began to build the tiny cigar that people were starting to call cigarettes.

Pistols were not common here, especially those worn in a fancy hand-tooled holster tied down to the thigh. The pipe was more common than those effete looking cigarettes. But there was something about the man as he stepped up to the bar. Eyes the color of clover and heavy brows gave the man a different look. He might have been handsome before the scar slashed his face from nose to ear. Whatever caused the scar hadn't missed his left eye by much. Johan's Angel of Death had looked aside that day.

There was no one else in the tavern this afternoon but a half dozen boarders were upstairs providing some welcome coin in exchange for a warm and comfortable shelter along with hot coffee and the wonderful bread Mrs. Mina had become famous for.

Emmanuel glanced at the younger man. His name wasn't important. He was neither a veteran nor a man Emma would ever invite to luncheon. The older man, though, there was something about that scar and he was of the right age to have served. There was also a poise and a way to how he moved. Combined with the hard used pistol butt evident in the holster Emmanuel would have wagered the man was a veteran.

"Rye if you got it," the veteran said, speaking with a smooth southern accent.

There had been plenty of southern men in the ranks of the blue, whole regiments from Missouri and men from every southern state had served under the right flag. Somewhere along the way Emmanuel had heard it said that a quarter of a million men of the south had served the US flag during the war. As far as he knew, most of those men would have been black.

Emmanuel looked at the man and studied him a moment then made a decision. "I wouldn't wish Johan's whiskey on Jeff Davis. Most of what we have is beer and some of Mrs. Mina's dandelion or rhubarb wine."

The man's eyebrows raised, though whether in irritation at the name Jeff Davis or something else Emmanuel couldn't have said. "Dandelion wine? I haven't had that in years."

Emmanuel nodded and poured a glass from the bottle behind the bar then drew a glass of beer for the other man.

"That'll be a dime," Emmanuel said before the man could lift the beer to his lips.

A dime slid across from the veteran.

"No, he pays, your first drink is free. Veterans are always fronted their first drink," Emmanuel said as he reached for a penny pipe and began to pack it.

"Even though I fought for the gray?" he asked.

Emmanuel snorted and pointed a thumb to the ornate mirror hanging behind the bar. "That mirror came from a Reb named Steven Cone that Johan did a good turn for. You fought. That's enough for me or Johan."

"Mighty big a' ya." He looked at the mirror as he sipped the wine. Then closed his eyes and let out a long sigh of pleasure. "I forgot how good this was. My grandma used to make it when I was little."

"Mrs. Mina makes it and sends a few bottles down here every year," Emmanuel said.

"Dandelion wine? Wine from weeds?" the other scoffed.

Emmanuel looked at him and shook his head. "The whiskey barrel had a rattlesnake and three plugs of tobacco dropped in for flavor."

Emma smiled as the young man turned slightly green. The veteran laughed. "I've drank worse."

"What Regiment? If I might ask?" Emmanuel asked.

"Cockrell's Missouri Brigade."

Emmanuel struck a lucifer on the match safe and lit the penny pipe. That action hid the measuring up of the man. What was he doing here? Missouri was a long way.

"Galvanized Yankee?" Emmanuel asked.

"No!" He answered sharply. "I was paroled at Vicksburg, never surrendered."

"Bentonville?" Emmanuel asked.

"No, Franklin ended the war for me." He motioned to the scar. A malicious look crossed his eyes. "How do you know I didn't kill any your friends?"

Emmanuel shrugged. "I'm as likely to have killed some of yours."

The veteran laughed again. "I suppose. Though I mostly saw blue coats running."

"All the way to Appomattox, then we stopped running. We only ever ran towards the fight," Emmanuel replied to the jibe.

"Well said; you were in the line instead of in the rear."

"I expect we shared some of the same mud and blood," Emmanuel said seriously.

"I don't doubt that," He said as he finished his glass of wine and set a silver dollar on the bar. "I think I'll try some of that rot gut."

Emmanuel shook his head but drew a glass of whiskey. As he set out the change on the bar the Veteran said, "Keep it; I'd like some information."

Emma panicked at the thought, but Emmanuel stayed calm. "Ask away, if I know I'll pass it on."

"Looking for a feller, goes by the names Jeffery Piper. Heard he had family up this way somewhere."

Emma sighed a breath of relief as Emmanuel scowled. "Piper? Can't say as I heard the name."

"Stands about yay high, usually wears a bowler hat. Likes to live beyond his means and has a lame right arm. That mean anything?"

Emmanuel pulled a wash rag out and rubbed a spot on the bar. "No, that doesn't really sound like anyone around here that I know of. Why you looking for him?"

"He's wanted for murder down in St. Paul. He kicked his wife to death and bashed his little girls head in." As he spoke he pulled a badge from his pocket and set it on the bar.

Emmanuel let out a long breath. "If I knew him I'd get the rope and organize a necktie party."

Johan chose that moment to step into the tavern. He brought a gust of cold air in with him. His eyes settled on the two men at the bar and he grunted as he set his bag and rifle down on the nearest table. He removed his old army coat and stomped his boots on the store floor, probably trying to get feeling back into his feet.

"Johan, these folks are looking for a man. Ever hear of somebody named Jeffery Piper around here?" Emmanuel asked.

Johan looked startled. "What, who?"

The lawman spoke in that southern drawl. "Jeffery Piper, he's wanted for murder. You know him?"

Emmanuel watched Johan's eyes and saw recognition of the name. Johan knew the name; Emmanuel had no doubt of it.

"Who did he kill?" Johan asked. The way he spoke... Emmanuel hadn't heard that tone of voice from Johan since the war.

"His wife and daughter," the lawman said.

Johan's head snapped towards the door to the stairs of the inn. He reached for his rifle. "When? Which daughter?" His voice had taken on a cold tone that Emmanuel hadn't heard in years and he felt fear rise up in his throat.

The lawman looked pleased. "His wife Cara and his daughter Kimberly, a month or so back in St Paul."

The looks that quickly crossed Johan's face were first one of obvious relief then sorrow followed by absolute rage. Emmanuel took a step to the side and dropped a hand to the Spencer rifle under the lip of the bar. That look on Johan's face meant men would die.

Emmanuel saw both the lawman and his companion furrow their brows; the lawman's hand slowly moved towards the pistol at his hip. Emmanuel shuddered and softly said, "His rage isn't at you; he knows the man and will see him dead."

The lawman's brow raised and his mouth dropped slightly as Johan reached up into the rafters and pulled down his old accoutrements. He set them on the table, then drew the wicked saber bayonet he had carried through the whole war from its scabbard and tested the edge. Johan looked at it a moment then looked to Emmanuel and the other two in the tavern.

"You speak of a dog we know as Jeff Sipes. His family lives on the third floor of this place." Johan spoke slowly and carefully but his accent was heavier than usual. "The wind is coming up too much and it is too late to get him today. I know where he will be on the morn."

"Sipes? You're sure?" Emmanuel asked, but Emma knew it to be true. There had been talk of the man having an ugly temper and Sherrie had once only poorly hidden a bruise. But murder? Emmanuel didn't think he had the balls. Then again, an unarmed woman and child might be his preference.

"I broke his collarbone last spring and told him he had best never return. If he *has* returned, I have a promise to keep." Johan's tone sent a chill down the spine of Emma and a weird thrill into the stomach of Emmanuel.

"I think a hanging party is in order," Emmanuel said.

"No, I have been tasked to bring the man to St Paul to face trial. I'll see no man hanged without a trial." The lawman spoke with the voice of command. He had given orders on the field of battle and it showed in his posture and tone. He expected to be obeyed.

"Your puppy can carry the rope and you can have him after he's hanged," Johan snarled, with rage behind his words.

"*No.* I saw too many guerilla hangings of unarmed men in the War. I will never again allow one in my presence." Again, that tone of command was there.

Johan looked into his eyes and the man did not flinch as many had before. "I'll let you know in the morning where he swings," he growled.

An icy calm voice came from the lawman. "No, I gave my word that I would uphold the law of this country. You will not be the man to make me go back on my word. No man ever will. I promised that Jeffery Piper or Sipes will stand before a judge and jury and pay for his crimes at the hands of the law."

Johan stared at him with an evil glint in his eyes then broke into a slight smile. "I will take you to him in the

134

morning. You will leave his family out of the papers; they deserve that. They are good people. You will promise me that, or you will never find him."

The lawman furrowed his brows and the scar along his face crinkled in the light from the fireplace. "Fair enough. We'll go in the morning. I never liked traveling in the snow. "What's your poison, I'll buy you a drink."

Mina stretched and took in a breath of the stale air in the inn. She was looking forward to spring and being able to leave the windows open for a good airing. Johan had built up a good fire in both the fireplace and stove of the inn. As a result the place was quite comfortable. She had no idea where he and Emmanuel had gone. They and the two boarders from last night had left well before dawn.

There had never been a lawman in the inn overnight before. His presence had calmed the boisterous and made the Sipes women a bit curious. The man had studiously ignored them but his companion had stared at the girls and their mother for quite some time. Pretty women had that impact on most men. It was a reminder of what she had in Johan. He stared at her like that once in a while but she had never caught him staring at other women in such a fashion.

From the talk around the dinner table it was clear the lawman, William Kerns, was a southerner that had worn the gray in the late War. No one seemed to mind, he didn't even receive hostile looks from Johan or Emmanuel. Though Mina herself had reservations about allowing him to stay the night in the inn. Freedom had decided the manner for her or anyone else that might have harbored similar reservations when she had unexpectedly crawled into the man's lap. She wasn't sure who had been more startled, her or Emmanuel.

He was a decent man from what she could see and she knew he kept looking out of the corner of his eye at Tisha and her daughters. The look was not one of lust, but curiosity. He was measuring them though not as a slave owner might a horse or slave. He was measuring them as a man might who was curious of how something so beautiful could be here, in this place. Neither Danielle nor Sherrie noticed but Tisha did. Shortly after dinner was ended she cleared the table and after dishes ushered her two daughters up the stairs.

Mina shook her head at that and her braid fell from her hair wrap. She swept it aside with annoyance and began repairing it. Kerns with his guide, plus Emmanuel and Johan, had left early in the morning. Emmanuel had taken his Spencer and Johan not only his old army rifle but the bayonet as well. That was unusual. It was cold this morning and there was no need to bring in any game, as Emmanuel had brought down a deer just two days ago.

She tucked her braid back into the head wrap as Freedom came out of her rooms with an enormous yawn. She was growing so fast. Mina looked at her with pride. She may not yet have been ten years old but she was full of poise and natural grace. There was an intelligence that gleamed from behind her dark eyes.

"Mama, will they bring the bad man back here?" she asked as she moved to the dry sink and picked up a cup.

"What? Freedom, what bad man?" Mina asked in confusion.

"The one Mr. Kerns called Jefferery Piperorsipes." She mangled the name but the name Sipes caught her attention.

"What? When did you hear that?" Mina demanded.

"Yesterday afternoon in the tavern." She answered in a matter-of-fact fashion.

"How did you hear that?" Mina was shocked.

"I was in the cellar reading," Freedom answered as she stated to prepare the coffee pot for the morning coffee.

"Reading?" Mina couldn't wrap her head around Freedom calling Jeff Sipes a 'bad man.'

"I had the copy of Milton. Emmanuel says it is too big a book for me."

Mina chuckled. "But why are they going to get the bad man?"

"He said the bad man killed his wife and daughter. Then he said Johan could not hang him." Freedom set the coffee pot on the stove and looked oddly at Mina. "I don't understand that. I thought bad men were supposed to hang so they won't hurt more people."

Mina was stunned at the question and at the maturity that could present such a question. "The law says there is to be a trial before a person can be sentenced to die."

Freedom shook her head and her bangs dropped in front of her eyes, she swept them aside in annoyance. "That doesn't make sense Mama. If everyone knows a man is a bad man, why do that?"

137

"That is the law, justice should be blind. People do not always know everything and sometimes the innocent look guilty," Mina answered patiently.

The men couldn't have left for Jeff Sipes, he hadn't been back since last spring when he stopped just long enough to pick up the horses... and everything of value he could get from their little house. Not to mention leaving bruises on all three of the Sipes women. No one had heard from him since and none had asked.

"But justice isn't blind. Indians don't get a trial," Freedom said with a furrowed brow.

Mina let out a sigh of exasperation. How could she explain the difference between an ideal and reality? Or of how skin color changed things in the eyes of the law? Freedom had been raised in a color blind home. How could she...

Sherrie skipped down the stairs interrupting Mina's thoughts. The dress Mina had made for her twirled around her ankles as she moved and hummed a tune. She did a little dance at the bottom of the stairs and the white trim at the bottom of her skirt spun nicely. Mina appreciated the distraction as Freedom ran to her and hugged her.

"Sherrie, why does Danielle stuff her corset?" Freedom asked.

Sherrie blushed and Mina choked back a laugh.

"Freedom, Danielle is growing. Just as you will." Mina said around a smile. "Now shoo, go do your chores, little angel."

Freedom did as instructed and ran up the stairs to do the distasteful job of emptying the chamber pots first. Then it would be bringing up a basket of firewood from the woodshed and washing up before breakfast. If Emmanuel were here she would help him feed and water the horses as well.

Sherrie watched Freedom run up the stairs out of sight. "Danielle does stuff her corset when she knows her beau is coming to call." Sherrie said with a slight smile.

Johan gritted his teeth as he slid the spill plane across the edge of the broken plank and watched the spill add to the other kindling filling the basket. It did not take him long. Freedom would come for the basket in the morning.

As he set the spill plane back in his toolchest he looked at the other tools within. A scribe, couple of hammers, one of them a fine English one. Two good plumb bobs on spools, spoke shaves, a pair of squares and a good brace with a variety of sharp bits. The saws looked sharp, as did the various chisels and carpenter's knife and other edged tools. He ran his fingers across several of the wood handles. A little oil might not be a bad idea. But not tonight.

Tonight... tonight he should have been having a good stiff drink celebrating the death of a man that beat on women and killed babies. Never in his life had he seen anything but pure cowardice in the thought of killing a child. An infant at that. The dirty son of a bitch had killed a woman as well. That he beat his own daughters and wife was bad enough, but killing a baby and its mother... his own wife! For that there was no forgiveness.

The law would deal with Sipes; Marshall Kerns had promised. But if the man failed to hang? What then? Who would speak for the dead then? Who cared enough to speak for them? The law was not blind and cared little for the black or Indian or the immigrant, especially the Irish. He should have hanged Sipes where he found him,

Marshall Kerns be damned. Johan knew he could have easily gathered a score of men to help if he had needed it. But he should have done it himself. He failed to keep his promise to Sipes, he should have hanged and buried him where he found him.

Johan shut the lid to the tool chest feeling rage welling up. He looked up at the two levels and plumb board he had set on the top of the stone wall. He took a deep breath feeling the chill in the air. He had a lot to think on. Should the law fail to hang Sipes, he would.

A bit of heat was leaking into the woodshed from the tavern, but not much. It was quiet, the last customers had left an hour ago and Emmanuel had gone to sleep on a table wrapped in his bedding with his old army greatcoat as a pillow. It was warmer than his room above the stable... It was cold tonight. Johan suspected it would be as cold or colder tomorrow. Everything also pointed to more snow. He could feel it in his bones.

He filled the basket with firewood and carried it into the tavern shutting the door with his boot. It was quiet with only a slight snore from Emmanuel. The only light was the lantern hanging over the bar and a feeble glow from the fireplace. The heat in the room was still good and he knew the rocks inside the tin bucket sitting on the floor would provide heat until nearly dawn when Emmanuel would wake to waken the fires.

Johan fed the fires in the stove and the fireplace. Then went up the stairs to the main floor of the inn. He smiled as the stairs announced his presence. The main floor was still warm as well, but wind rattled the north windows behind the heavy curtains Mina had made. He fed the fireplace and stove on this floor and made his way to the third floor.

Only three of the rooms were occupied by boarders and the Sipes women. It was coldest here, but the walls were built tight enough to keep the wind at bay, and the open stairwell let heat up the stairs from the main floor to take the edge off the chill.

The Sipes women were all sharing one bed under a pair of knitted afghans and two buffalo robes. A bed warmer full of hot coals had heated the bed before they ever climbed in. He thought there was likely a quilt or two as well. The others, three lumberjacks, were content in their beds with warming pans to keep them comfortable. At least they had yet to complain this winter.

Johan did his normal cursory check on the third floor and headed back down the stairs. A single candle provided the only light other than the glow from the fireplace in the common room. Mina had set the tin bucket full of hot rocks in the center of the common room. When the fist-sized rocks were heated to red hot and set in a tin bucket with another upended over it, they would provide about an hour of heat per rock. It was a trick he had picked up in... he tilted his head in thought. Was it in North Africa or the Crimea? He could not quite recall. But the practice had done them good service at Fort Abercrombie in the early part of the war.

Johan extinguished the candle and walked into Mina's rooms. Freedom was in bed with her cat and Mina. All were sound asleep. Freedom had curled up with her back to Mina and pulled the blanket up to cover all but her nose. Johan could not see the cat but could hear it purring. That cat had been with them since the death of Sebastian and had adopted Freedom. Johan chuckled to himself; that lucky cat was a survivor and smart enough to know who it had to keep happy.

Mina lay on her side with only her face visible under a nightcap and the buffalo robe pulled up almost to her ears. In the dim glow of light from the moon her face looked perfect to Johan. She was his angel. Maybe the best thing he had ever done in life was to pull her from slavery.

Johan sat down carefully in the folding rocking chair he had bought her in St Paul. She hadn't really liked it when he had set it in her rooms, but it had grown on her. She had two rocking chairs in these rooms. The smaller one had a swing drawer under the seat which Mina used to store some of her sewing supplies. Mina often sat in that chair sewing or knitting by the fire. He half hoped it was her favorite because he had gifted it to her. A year after they had opened the place, he had paid twelve dollars in town for a wagon load of furniture for the inn side of the business which included the nice desk and a smaller cupboard. Since then, he had added the two rocking chairs in her rooms and another for himself. He had to admit when he was sore from the weather he could sit and relax some in the rocking chair. The rocking motion eased his aches somewhat.

Mina shifted slightly in her sleep and he just stared at her for a few minutes longer then reached out and lightly caressed her smooth face. That beautiful face and the kind spirit within had changed him. He knew he was no longer the man he had been before he met her. He snorted and tried to imagine what he might have been like without her. Dead and buried in some ditch by now, most certainly. Possibly hanged by some lawman like that Reb Kerns. He lightly ran his fingers across her face again and smiled as she smiled in her sleep.

Johan walked back down to the tavern, failing to keep the stairs from squeaking. The bottle of cognac behind the bar called to him and he poured himself a glass. He considered how he had failed the poor girl Cara. She had borne a baby, but he could not think of her as anything but a child. She could not have been much older than Sherrie. He ground his teeth together in anger at that thought. Speaking but a few words to her, he had immediately liked her. She was young and full of life and hope for the future. Sipes had taken that from her.

What more could he have done? She would have been better off as a widow; he should have killed Sipes then or last spring instead of just breaking his collarbone.

Johan had been promised a copy of the paper that would tell of the trial. It would make the papers as it was not often a man killed a woman and child within sight of a priest, the only witness to the crime.

He packed and lit his pipe. The tobacco was drier than it should have been and burned poorly. He watched the red flare in the bowl as he pulled on the pipe. The smoke with the cognac relaxed him. But his mind kept working. Cara had been an Irish girl and a Catholic priest was the only witness to her murder. He thought on that. Not as many as he might have liked would be all that sympathetic to a dead Irish girl.

He feared some lawyer would conjure some legal magic to keep Sipes away from the rope. He hoped not, in fact he went so far as to ask God to give justice to Cara and her young child. But if the law failed her and her God failed her... he would not. Johan might face the rope; it would not be the first time. He was ready to meet the beautiful Angel of Death. He had been glanced at by her many a time before. Perhaps it was time to look into her eyes as she led his soul to be judged.

Justice
Spring 1874

In the summer of 1873, a plague of locusts ravaged the cropland of southern Minnesota. In the spring of 1874, the locust eggs hatched. Farm families lost everything; it created an economic depression that lasted through the end of the decade. Churches, businesses, and the governor himself raised funds to help the destitute. People helped each other. Those who could not find help fled the state.

Johan set the last foundation stone into place and stood up to stretch. The sun was finally beginning to drop below the horizon. It was still chill, but he could feel a warmth coming. Spring would be short, but the warmer weather it brought would be welcome. He looked at his work; it had taken far longer than he liked, but the foundation was set to the south side of what would be the school. The Sipes barn would make a good building for the learning and the addition to the south side would be a decent if small place for the teacher to live. He chuckled at that thought; he had lived in smaller barracks.

No less than twenty families had stepped up to raise money and do the work to transform this barn into a schoolhouse they could all be proud of. He had thought they would build a stairwell on the outside of the building to replace the simple ladder that had gone between the horse stalls and hay mow. But Ivan had went to work with a saw and an idea, putting a stairwell in instead. Vincent had gotten some men to work with lathing to eliminate the drafts from gaps in the walls. Korbel and others had enclosed the rafters to better keep out the weather. Now there was the equivalent of a dance hall where the hay mow had been and where horses had once stood were the walls for two school rooms.

A dozen men had gotten together to build benches for the children to sit. A slate board would be here in a week or two for the teacher to write on. If all went well, the lean-to that would be the teacher's rooms would be done by the end of summer. If every one of the families who had expressed a willingness to help could give a dollar a month, they might be able to pay a teacher a decent wage and stock the school.

Johan smiled with pride as he packed his pipe and lit it. He looked to his rifle leaning against the inside corner of his stoneworks. He had done as he promised and set the foundation. It was as good a work as he had ever done. Tomorrow he would go hunting.

The newspaper had said Jeffery Sipes and two friends were planning to go west in the spring and seek their fortune along the frontier with the Dakota Territory. From what Johan knew of the man, that was most certainly nothing more than tall tales. Though the kind to give a good first impression, once the attention was elsewhere, Sipes would fall back on old habits of laziness. The most real work Johan had ever seen the man do was clear pasture for his horses. He had made his women do all of the other work. He had cut and run as soon as it looked like there might be real work ahead of him.

Where would he really go? He dare not stay in St Paul for long; there were enough Catholics and Irish there that he might find himself on the wrong end of a set of boots some night. He was not the type to seek work among the timber camps to the north, either. Was he a skilled enough gambler to try his luck on one of the riverboats that plied the Mississippi? That was a possibility, he had heard the man had some talent at cards. Such a life was not always healthy, though, so Johan rather doubted that.

How would he hunt the man? The law had failed and justice would be up to him. The trial had been long and drawn out with the defense attacking the Catholics, the Irish and anything else they thought might distract. The bastard Sipes was free. There would be no rope, and so Johan had much planning to do, much thinking.

Minnesota was a large state with a growing population. Still, getting lost here was not as easy as one might think. He might be able to put some feelers out among fellow

veterans. The GAR had members all across the state...
but that would let it be known he was hunting the gutless
wonder, and he could not have that.

He sighed as he took a deep drag on his pipe. The tobacco
soothed him. It would have been better had he buried the
bastard when given the chance. But that was the past,
there was no use thinking on that too much. There were
enough ghosts there to fill a graveyard. The fact was that
Sipes would not change; he would make a mistake and
find that his luck had left him. How many more would
suffer before that time? How many more would suffer
before Johan ended him?

The wind picked up and pushed the cold back into his
bones. It was time to go home. Home, he looked down the
road at the inn and smiled as he puffed on the pipe.

It had been the better part of a decade now, and it was his
home. Mina cleaned and lived in it, making it hers, he had
built it and he worked to keep the place up and running,
everyone he cared for lived there now and had a stake in
it. That said something about the place.

Johan scratched his beard and thought a moment as his
fingers brushed the old scar. Was he really necessary?He
pondered that a moment...

'Ponder.' Who would have believed such a word would
ever even cross his mind? He knew he was not the man
who came ashore in Charleston so many years ago. Mina
had changed him, for the better, he thought.

Dinner would be soon on the table, and it was the turn
of Sherrie to read tonight. He smiled at that thought, that
girl had a voice on her. It was no wonder that a young man
was pining for her. Her face and those eyes would conquer
any man she wanted. Her older sister was no different. He
was glad the Moenning boys had taken a shine to them

both. If all went well there would be a dual wedding in a year or two.

Johan put the stone working tools and mallet in his tool bag and slung it, then picked up his rifle. He wanted to be there for that wedding. He wanted to see something good come of his actions in life and smiled as he imagined it. There was a little coin put aside, enough to help the two couples get started. Mina had already promised to knit them a pair of blankets.

Then his thoughts turned to the father of those two girls. How could something so vile produce two such wonderful young women? Clearly, they had gotten the goodness of spirit from their mother. Had he not had Mina, perhaps… he laughed out loud and shook his head at that thought. Had he not met Mina he would likely be dead by now or at the very least nowhere near the thought of settling down to a nice meal and a book reading after.

The thought of that good meal brought him back to the walk to the inn. A few hundred yards and he would be in front of the fire warming himself among a small host of lovely women. A glass or two of cognac after and some time behind the bar would settle him.

Emmanuel… Emmanuel. How to deal with him… or… Johan had suspected for a long time that something was wrong but had not truly put his mind to it until lately. For the longest time he had suspected Nate was a woman in the ranks but had never had reason to call out his suspicion. Nate had been a soldier who never stopped trying. After his death, Mina, Seth, and Emmanuel had washed his body and there had been no doubt Nate was no woman. After that, suspicion or even thinking of a woman in the ranks had not mattered. Any woman in the company had stood up as well as any man. But after… after, Emmanuel had fallen apart, growing more and more quietly mad as time passed. With the word of the death of Little Foot Emmanuel had simply… stopped. Even the nightmares had seemed to cease. Or at least grown quieter.

Then the letter from Kevin had arrived with the news that Emmanuel's father had resurfaced. The man had no idea who the hell Emmanuel was. He had spoken only of a daughter, Emma, who had run off just before the war. At first that proof had not mattered. Who was he to say anything about a woman who played at being a man?

Though 'played at' were not the right words. Emmanuel was a man. But who was Emma? Would some sort of split identity cause problems, more than were already there anyway? Did it matter?

Emmanuel poured a tankard of beer for Ivan just as Johan walked into the tavern, bringing a cold blast of air with him. It was well and truly past becoming annoying that Johan was out and about so much. The GAR, church, school and everything else he was involved with in the area made everyone aware of the tavern and the inn and drummed up business. Just by being present Johan reminded everyone where they could get a drink that wasn't watered down and was reasonably priced. By his assistance with a half dozen building projects around town, he had people who owed him favors. His involvement with getting the church and school set would garner him more favors owed.

As much as Emmanuel wanted to, there was no saying that Johan didn't do his share of the work and more. The man rarely slept more than four or five hours and the rest of that time he was doing something. Whether it was scouting deadfalls and hauling the wood back or doing repairs around the place. Most nights it was Johan that shut the place down, chasing the last customers out or laying a blanket over them when they'd passed out on the floor.

Emmanuel watched Johan carefully hang his greatcoat and gloves up to dry on a peg by the stove. It was still cold with more snow on the ground than anyone liked. The snow should have been long gone, but this year winter refused to let go and springtime was all but gone. Emmanuel sighed as the realization struck that they would have to get more firewood. The woodshed was near to empty and the remaining windbreak of wood was getting pretty thin.

Ivan accepted his tankard and took a swallow of his beer. "Thank you,"he said quietly in his heavily accented English. It was his free drink of the evening. He would buy at least five more before he wandered home through the snow. Emmanuel smiled as Ivan walked to the table he and Vincent always shared. Money was short in the area, but Johan insisted that the free drink for veterans was part of the business and would not be changed so long as he was involved in the place. It was the right thing to do.

Vincent and Ivan were the only two customers so far today. Another couple regulars might come in and the five boarders might come down from the inn after dinner, but who knew.

Emmanuel liked Ivan and Vincent as well as all of the other veterans who frequented the place, there were even a few who had not served that were tolerable. but with fellow veterans there was no need to pretend. His anger and disgust were like many others who had fought and hoped for something better to come home to. But countries didn't change, only the people. It was becoming harder and harder not to rage at those who hadn't served, the stay behinders and wannabe soldiers, and his hate and anger were palpable. Emma could all but taste it and sometimes complained. Only little Miss Freedom and her visits every day made any difference at all. Emmanuel smiled slightly as a chuckle came out; they should have named her Angel instead of Freedom.

Johan leaned against the bar and looked hard at Emmanuel. Emma was startled by his sudden appearance on the wrong side of the bar and froze for a second, the look in his eyes was unnerving. The man just stared a moment and weighed his words carefully before he spoke.

"I will need to go towards St Paul shortly," Johan said. "I know I can trust you to watch over Mina, Freedom and the other women." Johan rarely called them the Sipes women anymore, they were simply the women as though they were the only women in existence beside Mina.

Emmanuel's eyes closed unconsciously as a slow nod was given. Johan had the newspaper this morning with the mail. Sipes, or whatever his real name was, had been saved from a noose. Some lawyer had convinced the jury that Jeff Sipes and Jeffery Piper were not the same man who murdered a woman and babe in arms. It didn't matter that the Marshall, Kerns, had testified that he had heard the man confess to the crime or that a Catholic Priest had testified to witnessing the attack. Kerns was a former Confederate soldier, and the Priest was not only Catholic but Irish.

Johan had read the paper and simply went outside. He hadn't said a word, just leaned against the wall of the barn and stared into the distance for at least an hour. He'd also managed to skip the noon meal upstairs which was not something he often did. Now there was something behind those cold eyes and it shook Emma to her core and was more than a little unnerving to Emmanuel as well.

"You going to hang him?" Emmanuel asked.

"No, I promised that Reb lawman I would not hang the man." There was a glitter in Johan's eyes as he spoke. The man was going to die; the only hope was for Sipes to get out of the country... all the way out of the country. But Sipes was not famous for an overabundance of intelligence.

"Don't you get seen, that Marshall will know who did it as soon as word gets out Sipes is dead," Emmanuel said.

Johan smiled that frightening smile. "Dead? I heard tell the man went west where there is work. Haven't you heard the rumor that there is gold out that way?"

"Just you be careful," Emmanuel said around a smirk. If they had hanged the bastard when they caught him Emmanuel would have been glad to have been part of the hanging party.

"If you see him, do not hesitate to use your Spencer. You will be protecting the women of this place. He has no reason to ever again come near here."

"Will do, Sergeant," Emmanuel said without thinking. Johan sounded like the soldier who had survived the war again. Though, none but a fool would ever imagine Johan going soft.

Johan just looked at Emmanuel for a full minute. "Hand me my cognac; the bottle with the cross on it."

Emmanuel did as instructed and passed the bottle and a glass to Johan. Johan poured himself a half glass and replaced the cork. Then he just held the glass looking at the cognac.

"Emmanuel; anything happens to me, you take care of Mina and the girls. My share of the place will be split between you and Mina. I had it wrote up in town all legal like," Johan said quietly as his eyes took in Ivan and Vincent. "Vincent and Korbel witnessed it."

Emmanuel nodded somberly. "Alright."

"Do you remember the women soldiers wearing gray at Allatoona?" Johan asked.

The question was quite unexpected. Emma screamed at Emmanuel to be careful but Emmanuel was not in the mood for caution. "Yea, I think some Illinois boys buried one killed near the redoubt, and there was one or two in the hospital."

"I have done much thinking, perhaps too much. Those women fought well, as well as any man in the ranks. For the longest time I knew we had a woman in the company who was no laundress."

Emmanuel knocked the ash out of the penny pipe and packed it again in an effort to conceal the fear from Johan.

"There was no woman in the ranks."

"I had come to think it was Nate, not that I cared,"Johan continued as if he had not spoken. "Nate was a damned fine soldier. Then you and Seth cleaned him up after he died. I knew it was not him," Johan said as he packed his own pipe. "I thought I might have been wrong but then I remember one cantiniere from the Legion. If she had not worn a skirt, I doubt a man among us would have known she was a woman.

"She was as fierce a fighter as any man among us. I watched her brain two Russians with her barrel of brandy and kick another in the fork so hard he died later. There is nothing saying a woman cannot fight when the time comes. I am not one that holds that a woman does not deserve to fight if she must. I have known too many women that would kill."

"You going to suggest Sherrie or Danielle join the army?" Emma asked before Emmanuel could stop her.

Johan smiled wickedly. "No, those two are all woman. If they must they could kill; of that I have made certain. But they are not so bad off that they must pretend to be something else.

"You forget, I came of age in a brothel among women. I cleaned up after them, emptied their chamber pots. In future, do a better job of burning those bloody rags."

Mina set aside the newspaper from St Paul. That paper would send Johan hunting, and she could not say that he was wrong to do so. She could think of little worse than killing a child. Not even the worst men in the regiment would have stood by for such. The law had proven to be neither blind nor overly honest. She knew Johan would go looking for Jeff Sipes, and try though she might, she could not fault him for it. She tried to think of it from a Christian perspective, tried to forgive Sipes his crime but she just couldn't. Her opinion of Minnesota men had dropped like she never imagined. People had raised thousands to help those who had lost everything to the locusts but not a penny had been raised to bury a woman and child murdered by their man, and why? Because they were Irish.

Mina knew it was foolish to expect the law to be fair. The law wasn't fair to Indians or negroes. Why should the Irish be any different? So she wished Johan luck in his hunt; it wasn't very Christian of her, but…

How could he even find the man? Where could he even start to look? According to the paper, Jeff Sipes had declared that he would leave the state and seek his fortunes where he might not be mistaken for the despicable Jeffery Piper. The paper had never even mentioned his family here. Thank God for that, for they had no need to be associated with such a thing. If they had… Mina half expected there would have been a fire in those newspaper offices. Would that even have been a sin?

Tisha walked into the kitchen from the common room and stared at Mina for a moment. "Do you think my husband will come here?"

Mina didn't even think before answering. "He would be mad to do so. Too many know him and he knows Johan will shoot him on sight, as will Emmanuel… or I."

"He has nowhere else to go. There is the property here, and the girls and I." Tisha spoke looking out the window. She looked so small and lost.

"What could he do? You are here now with us. We will never let him harm you," Mina said quietly. "Johan and Emmanuel would kill for the three of you. You are family now and family takes care of family."

"You do not know him as I do. He is a hateful man who will seek revenge." Tisha said as she began to smooth down her calico skirt.

Mina chuckled darkly. "You have never seen Johan or Emmanuel fight. I will place the odds in their favor."

"I am Indian and you are black. The law cares nothing for us." Tisha said sadly. "He will strike at what Johan loves. He knows how to hurt and how to steal."

Mina stared at Tisha in silence for a few minutes. "Do you know what Johan has done for me?"

Tisha smiled and looked around the kitchen. "He brought you here and built this place of freedom and love."

"He plucked me from the auction block and gave me my freedom. He was the first white person to really give me a choice or care what I thought." Mina said as she pulled out the sourdough starter.

Tisha looked at Mina with those bottomless black eyes, the lazy eye seemed to look in another direction. Her pretty face looked sad. "He did the same for me and my children. The difference is that he loves you. At least so much as a man like that can love anything."

Mina didn't fully understand what she meant and put her confusion to words. "What do you mean?"

"Your Johan is a man who needs to... how can I say? To protect? He will do what he believes to be the right thing no matter who is hurt. He has seen too much to care about himself and will destroy himself to do what he thinks is right.

"Your Johan should have killed my husband when he had the chance. Now I think Jeff will come after us because we are the reason he was hurt. I should have killed him myself. Then no more children could have been hurt by him."

Mina stared at Tisha a moment. "Don't make the mistake of thinking Johan is a gentle soul. Johan will..."

Tisha interrupted, which was unusual. "My husband is not a man, but a beast who hates anything he does not control. He will kill us, and then you and Freedom. Your Johan will be alone."

Mina felt a little shiver go up her back at those words. "You never knew Johan as a soldier. He is a hard man who thinks he is only really good at one thing, killing. I have seen a few bad men in my life but Johan... Johan is the kind of man that frightens those kinds of men. Yet he has a soul that is good despite what he thinks."

Tisha raised the corner of her mouth in a sad smile. "That is the difference. My husband has no good in him. He is like a wasp nest, empty but of hateful wasps. Hate always wins."

"Well then. If Johan fails to stop him I have a Colt revolving shotgun for mad dogs like that. I will not pass quietly into the night, and neither will your girls."

Tisha smiled sadly. "I hope you are right."

"I am. Now hand me that string of turnips. Dinner tonight will have to be venison and turnip soup."

Vengeance, A Dish Best Served Cold 1875

The United States Congress passes the Civil Rights Act in 1875, which prohibits racial discrimination in public accommodations and jury duty. James Augustine Healy becomes the first Black Catholic Bishop in the U.S., and Alexander Graham Bell makes the first voice transmission.

$\mathfrak{J}$ohan set his hammer to full cock and placed the Sharps on the tree branch, letting the weight of the rifle settle into the crook of the tree. He would fire when his targets passed the dead scrub pine he had paced out at just under two hundred yards.

He had been trailing them for the better part of a week. Always careful to never let himself be sky lined and to stay out of sight. Yesterday he had let them pass in the morning so he could check their camp and verify what he knew and what he suspected. This had taken too long to allow himself any mistakes.

Their camp proved him right. Just four men and a wagon with four horses spread among them. They were failing to truly care for their horses, and the horses were tired. Two of the creatures needed fresh shoes and the wagon had a crack in the right rear wheel that made it easy to identify in the patches of snow. The wagon was a big one and it needed at least four horses or oxen to pull it. They could have hitched the other two horses to the wagon, but it was clear two of the men preferred to ride instead of walk. They had made just six miles yesterday. With more or better horses they might have made ten. While it was still chilly, winter was gone, the snow rapidly melting away. Another couple days like today it would be gone and with the way the winter had been, this spring would not be too muddy.

The talkative barkeep in Alexandria had told him they had said they planned to make for the gold camps of the Black Hills. No one else was planning to use the road for at least a week, and then it would be a family party of a dozen wagons and fifty souls. That wagon train was not going to overtake him or the group he followed; if they were unlucky, they would merely stumble across the remains and take caution.

His little copse of trees was close enough to the creek to do what he needed, for once the wagon crossed the creek they would make straight for the large cottonwood tree below him that was known on the trail as a good campsite. They would be coming straight at him with the setting sun in their eyes, with the only cover being this copse of trees or the shallow creek bed a half mile behind them. It would have been more difficult shooting had they followed the creek bed, but that would have added at least a mile to their travel and they were clearly tired and more than a little lazy. The right-hand rider was sleeping in the saddle and the left was a fool of the highest order. He had not even bothered to remove the saddle from his horse last night. Even if he failed to kill the four of them, the horse would be dead within the week. Never mind the Lakota village two days ride to the west, where a half dozen warriors might take interest in the horses. He would gift them the horses and whatever else of use in the wagon. The pair of shotguns and the two barrels of flour he had seen would be a welcome gift as well.

Johan settled the front sight of his Sharps on the chest of the left-hand rider. The man was tall and not thin, and the horse strained under the burden.

There were a half dozen paper cartridges to hand and Johan was using the pellet primer which allowed him to bypass putting a cap on the nipple. He was a good shot and if everything went well then no more than six or seven shots would be needed. If everything went right... things never went as planned. A soldier knew things were simple until it came time to kill. So, his old army cartridge box slung across his chest carried another forty rounds.

He felt the breeze from the west and it ruffled the leaves around him. A bird settled on the deadfall a few paces to his right. It stretched one wing out as though pointing away from him and made a bird sound that sounded like a question. It was an odd scene.

Johan gently caressed the trigger then took a deep breath to steady his breathing. When he squeezed the trigger the crash of the bullet traveling down range almost surprised him. It certainly surprised that bird who flew off like it was on fire. The bullet toppled the man from the exhausted horse and woke the sleeping rider.

Johan gave him no time to react. Though to the rider's credit, he had his shotgun in hand almost immediately. It did not matter because Johan had reloaded, and the man was in his sights. Before anyone could identify where the shot had come from, Johan was squeezing the trigger of the Sharps a second time. Either his shot was low and creased the horse's head or the man had laid spurs to his mount, for the horse took off running as the man tumbled off. The wounded or dead man dragged behind with a foot caught in the stirrup, and from the way he was bouncing about, he was not conscious. That was good; being dragged to death was no way for a man to die.

As he loaded his third round a shot came from the wagon, a carbine. He was well out of range of a shotgun and the carbine Sipes had bought was at best a hundred yard or so weapon. Much past that it was merely an accident to hit anything purposefully.

Oddly, the wagon continued towards him with the driver trying to coax the two tired horses into a run. That was foolish, as it only made Johan's task that much easier. It brought the dead men closer to him. Sipes did not jump from the wagon. Not that it would have mattered. There was no cover within a hundred yards of the wagon though he might have tried to use the wagon as cover.

Johan's third shot missed completely which surprised him and he let out a vicious oath as he reloaded. Watching Sipes frantically feed cartridges into his carbine, Johan shook his head in disgust. The damned fool was only just now loading his weapon?

His fourth shot knocked the wagon driver back into the interior of the wagon and from the way blood sprayed Johan knew his shot had hit true. The horses immediately slowed then stopped, hanging their heads in exhaustion. As it was, he doubted they could have gone much further than this little copse of trees.

Sipes chose that moment to finally jump from the wagon and race behind it. It had taken the man long enough to figure where the Angel of Death was coming from.

Johan finished reloading, and simply watched and waited. He could be a patient man when need arose. Picking up a stick of venison jerky he had set aside, he took a bite. A few minutes later he took a swallow of water from his canteen. Its taste was not terribly good, but it felt good as it slid down his throat. As he was setting the canteen down, Sipes sent a barrage of shots toward him, emptying the Winchester as fast as he could lever it. Johan was uncertain where the bullets landed, as none came close enough for him to tell. Sipes' damaged collarbone made it difficult to be accurate; what a pity.

Johan simply watched from beside his tree. This was not the first time he had killed from ambush. He had learned the lesson well in North Africa when a patrol he had been part of was set upon. One Kabyle with a rifle had played merry hell with the men of the patrol, killing three and wounding two others before disappearing into the desert.

Their muskets had been grossly outranged by that single rifleman sending death into them from afar. It had badly unnerved all of them. The Lieutenant had ordered them to fix bayonets and died for his trouble. His copain Remi had given the obvious order to take cover.

This was not that different. Johan had carefully chosen the ground. He had scouted it and knew the lay of the land well. The men he was killing today had no idea. And so it was not so much murder as it was execution.

Johan watched the scene below him. The horse of the first man he had killed had run perhaps a hundred paces and stopped. The one dragging its rider had run down towards the creek and was now drinking. It had lost its burden; the man did not move. Johan watched him long enough to know he was dead. He had died within sight of the open grave Johan had dug the day before yesterday.

He looked back to the wagon. He could see Sipes reloading his Winchester. It took him longer than Johan would have thought. Sipes should have spotted where he had fired from but Johan did not think he knew. He was stuffing a revolver into his belt and had thrown a canteen over his shoulder. He was going to make a run for it.

Sipes darted from the safety of the wagon running full out for the creek bed. He was faster than Johan would have thought but he was running in a straight line. Johan took aim, being careful to correct for the strong wind and to aim low. The sound of the shot once again surprised him. A moment later Sipes fell head long into the sparse grass and patches of snow. Johan watched the man roll onto his back screaming in pain.

Johan went and gathered the two horses, checking the dead men that had been riding them for any signs of life. Neither man was familiar and he had not really expected them to be. Leading the horses to the wagon and its horses, he tied them to the wagon. There was no doubt the driver was dead, blood had sprayed across the canvas above where the driver had sprawled. Out of habit he took a quick look into the wagon to be sure and froze. The dead man was not a man at all, but a young woman wearing a dingy brown skirt. Her hands were wrapped in rags and bloody from a long time holding the reins of this team of horses.

"Merde!" Johan snarled as he climbed into the wagon and stepped across jumbled bedding and a pile of small boxes.

His shot had caught the woman in the throat, tearing it away. Death had been quick; at least the Angel of Death had spared the woman that. In life she had been plain but young. He doubted she had seen more than fifteen summers. Rage coursed through him. That damned fool Sipes had led another woman to the Angel of Death. Johan hopped from the big wagon and landed heavily. He leaned his back against the wheel with the crack in the tire.

Johan just leaned there a few minutes listening and feeling the rage well up inside of him, giving a red tint to everything he looked at. He snarled as he heard a faint moan in the distance.

Johan walked up on Sipes with his Sharps in hand. Sipes was sprawled on the brown grass, his head in a clump of snow. Johan's shot had struck the man low as intended, likely severing his spine. The man was crying and whimpering from the pain, but he was conscious.

Johan pulled the revolver from Sipes' belt and looked at it. A quality cap and ball Remington such as the cavalry had carried. It was in good shape. When he had fallen, the Winchester had gone muzzle first into the snow. Johan picked it up and looked it over, wiping away the snow as he did so. He did not like the feel of the weapon, perhaps because Sipes had owned it.

Johan stood there looking down at Sipes. He said nothing and just stared for a while.

"Kill me. Please," Sipes whimpered. His blue eyes blood-shot and his once handsome face blanched a stark white from the pain.

"No," Johan said simply and walked back to the wagon.

There were perhaps another two hours of sunlight then a full moon tonight. More than enough time and light for what he intended.

He fashioned a simple drag blanket from the blood-stained wagon canvas and dragged a screaming Sipes to the grave he had dug. Sipes was unceremoniously rolled into the hole in the ground. The grave was all of five feet deep and wide, meant for four men. It had taken him the better part of a morning to dig it and he had freely used the pickaxe he had brought along. The ground had only been frozen down a few feet but it still had been hard digging. He figured by the end he had moved the better part of five tons of dirt. The grass roots had been deep, some going at least the length of his arm.

Sipes screamed as he landed at the bottom of the grave cursing Johan's existence with every agony-filled breath. Johan said nothing as he dropped the other two dead men on either side of him. He listened silently as the man switched to begging for mercy.

Johan gently wrapped the dead woman in a large calico blanket and laid her atop the others in the grave. He was careful to leave space around Sipes head so he could breathe a while yet.

Then Johan silently began to fill the grave, listening to Sipes curse, scream, rail against life and finally beg. None of it bothered him. Johan had seen death in all of the horror man could imagine and had done some of it. He had killed and murdered before. Right now, his heart was as dead as ice. He might not even have felt the cold rock in the pit of his stomach, but for the young woman.

Johan threw down a ratty blanket he had found in the wagon and let it fall across Sipes' hate and terror filled face.

"Hurry on ahead; hell is but half full," Johan said, as he filled in the rest of the grave, entombing Sipes in his grave of terror. He listened to the quieting screams as dirt filled the hole and silenced forever the waste of a man Johan had known as Jeff Sipes.

Johan looked at the simple marker he had set with the words burned into the board with a running iron he had made from a broken cinch pin. A simple thing, more than was present for most buried on the prairie, it would guarantee no one would blame the Lakota, as they would have left the dead for the coyotes.

DED of POX
4 Sols
1875
Nown but to God

It had taken him some time to decide on the wording... any threat of the pox would keep people from digging up the grave for loot, only to find bullet wounds.

Johan set enough rocks to keep the coyotes from getting too curious and spent a while emptying the wagon of what might be of value. Loading the four horses as pack animals and gathering his own, he headed west toward the Lakota camp he knew lay there.

Johan raised quite a stir when he rode into the camp. Seven teepees in a circle with their doors facing east. He rode in just before dawn whistling a marching tune he remembered from the Legion.

The two boys watching the small herd of horses had alerted the braves and eight superb warriors on horseback waited for him just outside of their camp. He rode a good mare leading a pack mule and four horses. All but the mare were set with packs, a decent load on each.

The warriors looked at him with no expression on their faces. Thankfully, none wore war paint though he had no doubt all eight men would kill him in a blink. He could see several women and a couple children; none hid from his eyes. There was no fear here, but more than a little curiosity was evident. Not many sane white men rode into Lakota country alone.

The warriors were all well-armed. One warrior had a Colt pistol in hand, another a well-cared for Smith carbine, a third a Sharps carbine that had been shortened at both ends in the way favored by the Lakota and Cheyenne. A fourth held a Henry Rifle that had seen better days, with a scalp hanging from a sling swivel. That scalp was likely that of the original owner. The others carried lances.

Johan sat his mare saying nothing for a few minutes. Then in careful Lakota: "I come bearing gifts for the family of the warrior Little Foot."

The warrior with the cut down Sharps looked surprised.

"Why?" he demanded in halting but strong French.

Johan looked at the man harder for a moment and saw something familiar. He had met this man before, though he knew that had to be unlikely.

"I fought beside him; he was my friend, and I would see his family better off," Johan said.

"Crazy man who gifts small knives, why do you come to this place? Little Foot died among the Oglala far to the south," The man demanded. The others looked on with some curiosity.

"You are here now; I had hoped his kin might be near here," Johan said, hating the lie as he gave it. "I know this place."

"Little Foot had no family with the Lakota. He died fighting with Red Cloud against the long knives."

"He died well," Johan said. It was not a question.

The warrior with the Sharps smiled slightly and the man with the Smith shifted his horse looking at the pack horses.

"Did you come to trade pots and pans for buffalo robes again?" The man with the Sharps demanded sharply.

Johan laughed darkly and shook his head as realization came to him. "You were not yet an accomplished warrior then. I have nothing to trade today. I bring only gifts for you and your families to honor my friend Little Foot."

Johan dismounted and pulled a beautiful pipestone pipe in a red velvet bag from his pack mule and handed it up to the warrior with the Sharps.

"I wish to make certain I do this correctly. I bring gifts to give in memory of a fallen friend," Johan said.

Next, he moved to the lead pack horse and pulled the two barrels of flour down. The tired horse noticeably appreciated it. He added a barrel of salt pork, a bag of sugar, an all but new axe, pick and shovel to the growing pile.

Then a box full of metallic cartridges for the Winchester, powder, shot and caps for the shotguns as well as three decent pocket-knives, a good quality butcher knife and a decent camp hatchet. Then he tossed the four boxes of caps and cartridges for the pistols into that box. He looked up at the surprised faces and wide eyes of the warriors.

"The four horses are further gifts worthy of a son of Chief Bald Eagle. They are tired but will grow strong again."

Johan moved to his pack mule and pulled out a bag of tobacco and two small bundles of sage wrapped in a red neckerchief. He handed these last two gifts to the warrior holding the Smith. All of the warriors had dismounted and were looking at the gifts. Half a dozen children had appeared from nowhere and he fished out the bag of rock candy and divided it among them. He then pulled out two deer hides he had cured over the last few weeks and placed them on the pile of gifts.

"May I have the honor of your name?" Johan asked the warrior with the Sharps.

"I am Fast Horse." The brave said with a slight smile.

"Fast Horse; these last gifts require a gift in return. All I ask is to share a meal and to listen to the stories you might tell of my friend Little Foot. I might share some as well."

Johan pulled the canvas bundle from his pack mule and carefully set it in front of the braves. It took him a bit longer than expected to untie the knots he had made in the dark. He carefully unrolled the bundle being sure never to touch the weapons inside.

The Winchester immediately caught the eye of Fast Horse. All looked at the other weapons within. The two shotguns, Remington Army pistol and the small Colt pocket pistol he had found in the wagon were a considerable increase to the arsenal of this small band.

Emmanuel finished stacking the afternoon wood splitting. It was an absolutely beautiful day. Warm with a light
west wind and a cloudless sky. A good stretch and a cup
of coffee were in order before the tavern opened. Ivan and
Korbel had a celebration planned and were hoping the
half-dozen colored folk in the area would come. Congress
had made the Civil Rights Act official and President Grant
had promised there would be more to come.

As far as he was concerned, that was the first good news
in quite some time. Johan had been gone for more than
two months now and both Emma and Mina were beginning to worry that he was dead. Although in all honesty
Emmanuel had begun to wonder if he had just left for
good, abandoning everything in favor of his one-man
hunting expedition.

Both Danielle and Sherrie had started full-on courting
the Moenning boys, and they did so with the full approval
of Mina and Freedom. Their mother didn't seem to mind
either; though the opinion of Freedom and Mina was what
was most important.

Emmanuel started at the sound of the well house door
banging shut, and turned to see Johan walking with a
bucket of water towards a tired-looking mare and mule.
Johan had obviously already removed the saddle and
packs as both animals were simply tied to the hitching
rail in front of the water trough by the stable. He began to
wash and rub down both animals as they drank.

Emmanuel simply watched. When Johan finished the
grooming, he set the wooden bucket inside the well house
and turned the animals loose in the small pasture across
from the stable. He slung his Sharps rifle, picked up a set

of saddlebags, and a wooden lock box. The way he moved was not what Emmanuel expected to see. He was slightly hunched as though his back bothered him and his customary quick movement was not present today.

"Afternoon," Johan said simply as he stepped past Emmanuel into the tavern.

Up close the man looked terrible. His eyes were sunken and he had more gray in his unkempt hair and beard than when he had left, and both were heavily overgrown. He had also lost weight, as his clothes hung loosely from him in an odd manner.

Emmanuel followed Johan into the tavern and watched as he put his rifle in its customary place in the rafters and tossed the saddle bags onto the bar.

"There is a pair of moccasins and a beaded belt for you in there. Put the money in the till. We had a good month.

"I put a buffalo blanket in your room to use next winter if you've a mind to." Johan sounded tired and worn like Emmanuel had never heard him.

For the first time Emmanuel got a good whiff of Johan. He had clearly bathed before he arrived but he still smelled heavily of horse and desperately needed a visit to the barber. He had likely cleaned his threadbare clothing by laying down in a spring. His boots were badly in need of repair, if not outright replacement. And there was something else about him, something wrong. His eyes were dead, deader than Emmanuel had ever seen them.

"Welcome home, Johan, I'm glad you're back. Mina has been worried something awful about you, and all the girls ask after you every day. They're all at a church social. I don't expect them back for another couple hours," Emmanuel said, not quite sure how to ask if his hunt had been successful.

Johan nodded his head absently. "I did not know it was Sunday today. Lost track of the days some time ago." He looked at the bar for a moment and sighed.

"Pour me a glass of my cognac, would you? Then I will go to sleep. Please ask the girls to wake me when they return. I have not seen a bed in two months."

Emmanuel pulled Johan's glass down from the rack over the bar and poured a healthy measure from one of Johan's personal bottles of cognac. When he set it on the bar in front of Johan the man just stared at it a moment.

"Fill the glass," Johan said quietly. Emmanuel did so.

"Did you find..." Emmanuel started to ask but Johan simply waved the question away with a sharp gesture.

"I will not go west again in this lifetime," Johan almost whispered. "If I never again ride a horse, it will be too soon," he added sharply, then emptied the glass in one long pull.

"I need sleep," he said then as he upended the glass on top of the bottle and took the lock box and cognac bottle with him up the stairs. He stopped just before going up.

"Make sure the girls wake me for dinner. I have not had a truly good meal in a while... and I think I would like to see them again."

"I will," Emmanuel answered simply. Emmanuel had seen Johan tired before but never like this. There was more there than simple exhaustion. Something had changed.

Johan almost stumbled going up the stairs and he was so light of foot that the customary squeak of the stairs was absent.

Emmanuel let out a long breath and Emma whispered, "Good Christ, but that man terrifies me." Emmanuel did not disagree.

The saddlebags did indeed hold a beautiful set of moccasins that were incredibly soft and heavily beaded with a design he did not recognize. The belt was made from snakeskin and beautifully beaded as well. The other side held a bag of cheap tobacco, a couple penny pipes and a large pigskin bag. Emmanuel opened the bag and dumped it on the bar.

"Sweet mother of Jesus!" Emmanuel gasped. There had to be the better part of a thousand dollars there in gold coins and folding money. There was also a pair of gold teeth and a fine silver cross the size of a large key. Emma cringed at the sight of the teeth and cross.

All of the money went into the till. Counting it, there was closer to two thousand dollars, plus the deed for the Sipes place. That was all the answer Emmanuel and Emma needed as to the fate of the murdering bastard Jeff Sipes.

Mina opened the door to the inn and set the basket on the table in the common room. The scent of a fire in the stove told her Emmanuel had started a fire for them, even though it was warm enough outside that he really hadn't needed to. Then she smelled the coffee. That was odd, she didn't drink coffee all that often anymore since tea had become available from the general store last summer. There were no boarders at the moment either.

Danielle and Sherrie appeared, with Freedom between them. She smiled at the sight of them. Freedom was growing into such a beautiful child. She was ten now, and brighter than most adults. The reality was that she viewed both Danielle and Sherrie as sisters, and Tisha as an honored aunt.

Tisha screwed up her nose. "Who made coffee up here?"

Mina shrugged. "Emmanuel, I expect. They are hoping for a large crowd for the celebration tonight. Some will want coffee instead of beer or spirits."

Freedom skipped into their rooms and stopped abruptly. "Mama, there is a strange man sleeping on the floor," she said as she froze in the doorway.

Wonderful. A boarder came in while they were away and didn't know where to go. She strode to the doorway ready to wake the stranger and send him to a room upstairs. It took her a heartbeat to realize it was Johan laying on the floor next to the bed. He was asleep more soundly than she had ever seen him. She had never known him to not wake when the door opened, let alone allow two people to stare at him. Then she saw the brandy snifter and the empty bottle of cognac next to his old copper handled tin cup. She had seen that bottle last week when she dusted and it had been more than half full.

"Freedom, go help the girls get dinner started. I'll get Johan into bed," Mina said quietly.

Johan had set a folded blanket under him and simply laid down on it still in his clothes. His boots were badly in need of repair and there were at least two patches on his trousers. A heavily used penny pipe was held by its stem in one of the button holes of his jacket. His chest rose and fell as he breathed but he looked a shadow of the man who had left just over two months ago. His cheeks were hollow under his unkempt beard, his eyes looked sunken and there were dark rings under them. His eyes moved under their lids, telling Mina he was dreaming. There was a smell... fresh soap, horse and liquor.

Mina couldn't ever remember seeing Johan drunk, she knew she had never smelled liquor on him like this before. She just stood there watching him sleep for a minute, then knelt down and took off his boots. A boot knife she had never seen before fell to the floor and she set it aside. When she pulled off the other boot, he stirred slightly but didn't wake. Or at least she didn't think he did. His socks were more hole than fabric, and from the calluses evident Johan had spent a lot of time walking since he left. He had clearly bathed recently, as he did not stink and his clothes were clean, or at least mostly so, but the time away had left marks upon him.

She lifted him up by the shoulders, saying, "Get into bed, Johan. You don't need to sleep on the floor. This is your home."

"Ikverdiengeenengelzoalsjij," Johan mumbled. Or, at least that was what it sounded like to Mina.

He collapsed onto the bed and rolled onto his side away from her. "Ikhebcadeautjesvoor je op de stoel," he mumbled again.

"What?" Mina asked not understanding. It sounded like his Dutch but she had never learned it. She probably should ask Freedom to translate.

"La boîte sur la chaise berçante," Johan said in French.

He was drunk; she couldn't think of ever having truly seen him drunk. Mina had no idea what to say, but she understood the French reference to a box on the rocking chair.

She looked and immediately saw the wooden box he must have meant. She opened the simple catch and inside were five pigskin bags. In his scrawling hand names were written on each. A small bag marked Freedom was on top, Mina lifted it and looked inside. A pair of gold double eagles sat nestled on top of a small leather-bound copy of Voltaire.

176

She pulled up the largest when she saw her name on it. Inside were five double gold eagles, a fine silver pocket watch that needed to be wound attached to a chatelaine along with a small purse, silver comb, mirror and pen knife. An ornate inkwell and silver pen were there as well. But the presence of the card scraper, large pocket knife and spoke shave made no sense to her.

She looked again at the box and saw a piece of paper folded into the lid that had been written in his heavy hand. She picked it up and gasped.

"If I do not return by July 4 send this to Mina Steele. My last will and testament has been filed at the county courthouse. Tell her I have met the Angel of Death.

Johan Steele"

Mina just stared at the letter. He really had been prepared to die.

Violence Solves Nothing
1876

George Armstrong Custer and a large part of the 7th Cavalry was annihilated at the Little Big Horn on June 25th, and the United States Centennial was celebrated July 6.

mmanuel smiled sourly at the newspaper; it was another story about that damned fool Custer. Nothing interested Emmanuel past the first few lines, and the paper was folded and tossed onto the nearest table. The Centennial was over and the odds were that New York Democrat bastard Tilden was likely to win the presidency in November. The world really was going right into the sinks. If the Democrats were to win... then reconstruction and anything good it had accomplished for the black man in the southland was done.

Everything accomplished in four years of hell would be for nothing. Emmanuel cursed under his breath and looked at the two patrons sharing the table by the open door. Johan could be seen splitting wood in the yard. The rhythmic sound of a splitting maul was calming. It reminded all that heard it that the work was never done.

Emmanuel packed a penny pipe and lit it. The tobacco was too strong and stung Emma's eyes for some reason. After a couple pulls from the pipe Emmanuel put it down and let it go out. It was just too much today.

"Say Emmanuel, can you settle an argument for us?" Young Jim Lowe asked. The man was just now seventeen and strongly built. He was working at the local land office now as an apprentice surveyor.

"Yeah, maybe," Emmanuel said from behind the bar.

"You mnd the Steeles set this place up back in '66 when you came back from the War, right?" He asked.

Emmanuel gave a nod of the head. "Yes."

"Were there any womenfolk out here then?" he asked.

Emmanuel felt the lips purse slightly. "Just Mrs. Mina and Freedom. I think the Moenning women came later when the homestead was set. But I don't remember for sure."

The other man furrowed his brows. "What about the other three Steele women. Those are all Johan's kin right?"

Emmanuel smiled widely. "Depends on who you ask around here. But they're family. Mrs. Mina treats them all like her kin and Johan just calls them the Steele family."

Jim chuckled and raised his glass to Johan's back in the yard. "That man sure can collect pretty women."

"Hush that kind of talk," the other man said quickly. "If he hears you, he will read to you from the book. And God help you if one of the Moenning boys hear that." Then he looked to the bar. "He didn't mean nothing by that, Emmanuel."

"Jim, that better be the beer talking," Emmanuel warned with a grim look. "Otherwise, you'll find yourself out on the stump under Johan's axe."

Jim blushed hotly. "I didn't mean it like that!," he protested. "I meant he has a lot of pretty women in his family."

Emmanuel smiled now. "Mrs. Mina is married to him; Tisha is talking to Ivan, and Danielle and Sherrie are courting the Moenning boys. They're all spoken for and don't you be forgetting that. Any one of them would turn you to glue for even thinking ill of those women."

"But that ain't what I meant! I mean to say pretty women just ain't that common out here. Hell, women in general ain't! To see the old man with that many pretty women in one place is just plain strange. It's like all the pretty women in the county live in one place." He sighed and shrugged his shoulders in frustration. "I just mean that man is lucky
181

is all. He's got this place, all those pretty women and the rest of us... well we don't."

Emmanuel laughed. "You aren't wrong. You know I don't think I saw a dozen pretty women through the whole war. And next to Mina or Seth's sister Carlie, not too many were really that nice to look at."

The other young man nodded his head in agreement. What was his name? Another foreign immigrant from the continent, a young man maybe twenty years old. Vetch or Vitech or something odd like that. His English was really pretty good, with only the slightest hint of an accent.

"In the old country there are pretty women in every village and you can get a wife by offering her father some good livestock and the promise you would care for her. But if you have nothing to give... well, all a man can do is to look and hope. I came here for the promise of land. When I want to marry and make a family, I will write home to my father and ask him to send me a pretty bride."

Emmanuel just stared at him and felt his head shake. Emma silently called the man an idiot.

"You don't approve?" Jim asked. "Sounds like a good way of doing things to me."

Emmanuel just kept shaking his head. "That's no way to win a good woman. You better hope your father likes you or you'll get some old spinster."

The foreigner laughed. "Just so long as she can cook!"

Emmanuel smiled at that. "A good cook can make just about anything better."

The MacGowan brothers chose that moment to walk through the open doorway. Tully and Desmond had come from Illinois last spring with a small herd of cattle. They had set a homestead and built a barn and a house for themselves and were now building a second house. They were hoping to bring their families out in the next year or two if things went well. Tully had a daughter and a little boy that he bragged about regularly. Desmond had a young wife and had proudly shown a tintype of her around when he arrived. As far as either Emmanuel or Emma was concerned the picture showed nothing more than a pretty child with striking eyes. She didn't look much past twelve or thirteen.

"Tully, Desmond. When are you bringing your families out here to live?" Emmanuel asked.

Desmond tilted his head to the side and considered. He had deep blue eyes the color of seawater. Tully's eyes were as green as clover. Neither were ugly men but there was something about them that Emma disliked, and Emmanuel didn't disagree.

"I dunno, 'spect maybe in the spring. We should have the property done up nuff for the family and my boy Kyle should be out'a nappies by then. Why?"

Emmanuel smiled viciously and motioned to Jeff and his companion. "These two are taking an inventory of all the womenfolk in the county. Only counting the pretty ones."

It was a mean thing to do. Jim and his companion weren't looking for a fight, but Emmanuel had just put them squarely in the sights of the MacGowan brothers. The brothers had a reputation for having a temper.

There hadn't been a fight in the bar in a long time. Emmanuel liked to see the young men who were full of themselves go at it hammer and tongs. It might be nice to see Jim and his buddy with some missing teeth and a new more appealing color around their eyes.

Mina finished wiping down the table and looked out the window at Johan. He had spent the morning splitting and stacking firewood. It was always a yearlong project to restock the wood pile for the winter, a never-ending task like the laundry and the dishes. She would rather do the dishes any day than work the wood pile.

The long winter and Johan being away had also depleted the stock of beer and spirits in the tavern. The beer had nearly run out and some of the regulars had taken to drinking the poison Johan called whiskey. Some claimed to even like it. Johan was planning to go to St. Paul soon to get his stocks resupplied, and with the train now coming into town that would take considerably less time. It was hard to believe the trial of Jeff Sipes was two years gone now.

Before Johan had come back last spring, the newspapers had run a story about how Sipes's lawyer had been set upon by a pair of Irish toughs who had beaten him severely. The man had talked about how a dozen men had set upon him but the woman who ran the boarding house near where it had happened said there were no more than two and it might have been only one. The scum had it coming but the newspaper had used it as yet another excuse to vilify the Irish and described the lawyer as a saint.

Johan was finally looking better than he had when he returned from his last hunt for Sipes. She wanted to believe he hadn't found the man, but something had changed in him. She suspected Sipes was dead and it had not been a pleasant death. Though she knew Johan to be a hard man, as he always had been, there was a difference now. New lines around his eyes, he slept less... it was as though he had most thoroughly died inside and not even his cognac brought him respite.

184

She had never seen him drunk before he returned; now he closed the bar every night, and slept on it as often as not, rarely sharing her bed anymore and only caressing her face when he thought her asleep. But at least he never smelled of liquor or drank straight from the bottle.

He was spending less time in the inn, avoiding the girls, and Freedom would leave the room as soon as he entered. Johan had never been close to Freedom, but... Mina knew he loved her and still adored the girls. She knew he still loved; at least as much as he was capable of love. She loved him and that was what mattered. He was her man and would be until one of them was buried and then she would see him in heaven... whether he liked it or not.

Freedom tugged at her sleeve to get her attention and Mina started. She hadn't heard her enter the kitchen.

"Mama, why does Sherrie call Johan father when he is not able to hear but Johan when he can?" Her voice was turning and she was growing so fast. She wasn't twelve yet but she was already a beauty.

Mina smiled and stroked Freedom's hair. "Why do you ask such wise questions?"

Freedom's dark eyes looked up at her. "Because I can."

Mina laughed. "Because when Sherrie sees Johan, she sees the man she wishes was her father."

"Yuck! Then Tisha would be his wife instead of you and Ivan would be courting you!"

Mina smiled dryly but did not correct her. Had Johan not taken her from that slave market in Charlestown would she not still be in the hell of South Carolina?

"Sherrie calls him father as a form of respect. She knows her father is gone forever. Sherrie and Danielle both do it.
185

It's the same reason Tisha calls him brother and me sister. It stops questions; otherwise, people might talk."

"But Mama, people already talk."

"What?"Mina asked in surprise.

"The pastor says he is a man no better than he has to be. And his wife calls him a 'nigger keeper.'"

Mina felt her face flush in anger. She had thought better of the man. Though she wasn't surprised by the words of his wife. Perhaps it was time to look for a better church.

She looked out the window as Johan began splitting wood again. The axe rose and fell with a loud whack and he tossed the split pieces towards the pile. If he heard such talk there would be violence.

"Freedom, don't tell Johan about such talk."

"I won't, but the pastor calls him a devil." Mina ground her teeth and Freedom looked at her with concern. "Mama?"

"Freedom, don't you ever listen to such talk," she said severely.

"Why not? He doesn't deny he has killed and the Bible says thou shalt not kill. And Mrs. Bendon says if I follow the Bible and distance myself from evil men I can come work for her. Then I can make money to help you and maybe even make a good lady's maid."

Mina saw red for a moment and had to set down the dough knife she had been cleaning for fear that she might bend it.

"Freedom," she began, then paused. With a sigh she considered what to say, and how to say it best. "That is not the talk of a godly person," she continued. "That woman is ignorant. She only speaks one language and can't figure the church books without help. You are already better

186

educated than she will ever be. You and I can speak three languages; she speaks but one, and her words drip poison."

Freedom looked both surprised and offended. "I can speak four... that means I'm better educated than her?"

"Yes, though educated people can still be fools. You are not, and your education is not done. You will be no lady's maid. I will see you educated so you don't have to be. You have much to learn but you are already wiser and will be a better woman than she can ever hope to be."

"But the pastor says women, especially colored women, should know their place. I should learn to sew and keep house to..."

Mina interrupted her. "Does he now? We will not set foot in that church again, then."

She knelt down and grasped Freedom by the shoulders. "Freedom, Johan helped to build that church. He set the foundations and was there to raise the roof. We have been attending every Sabbath since it was a tent under that oak tree. I thought better of them."

Mina paused a moment and took a breath. "If Johan hears such talk bad things will happen. I want to burn the place, and that is not a Christian thought."

Freedom stared at her, wide-eyed. That was not how she had ever heard her mother speak. It was not how she should hear her mother speak.

"Mama... are the Bendons no better than they should be?"

Mina looked into those bottomless eyes and huffed. "Did the Bendons, or anyone else step up to help your sisters when they were in need? No, it was Johan and this family who fed them and saw them through that winter. Was it the Bendons who tended the Moenning family when they were sick? Were either of the Bendons there to build the school? No, it was those they have the audacity to talk ill of."

Freedom stared at her for a minute. "Mama, I am sorry. I thought they were people of God, and I should listen to them."

"The devil knows the Bible better than any preacher," Mina said quietly.

Johan sat on the grass of the hillock on the other side of the road from his place and enjoyed the breeze against his neck. It was hot and he was tired. He had spent a good part of the morning and part of the afternoon splitting wood with the new splitting maul he had picked up last week.

He packed his pipe and lit it as he watched Danielle, Sherrie and Freedom hang the laundry out to dry. There was just something peaceful about watching women set out laundry on a line. The wind played with their hair, and that both Danielle and Sherrie were absolutely beautiful did not hurt. Freedom was growing into a lovely young woman as well. She would be as beautiful as Mina, if not more so.

The three of them began playfully tossing a washcloth back and forth and their innocent laughter brought a smile to his face. Danielle and Sherrie were good women and would make good wives. Their background did not matter, and they were one more good thing he had done in his life. It would take a lot to offset the evil he had done, and when it came time to be judged there was going to have to be a lot more to balance the scales. He chuckled darkly to himself; if ever any deed of his could.

He frowned at the memories just under the surface and felt a shudder as one washed over him. The shudders were something new, and always came before a memory and those memories were not pleasant. The brutal cold of the Crimea would ripple across his skin, the cloying dust of North Africa, but the one that would almost drop him to his knees was the still, plain face of the woman he had killed. He had never killed a woman and had been proud of that. What did he have any right to be proud of now?

At least his cognac could dull the pain of his memories. He snorted at that thought: the pain of memory. What was he thinking? He had seen men gut shot who spent days lingering on in agony waiting for the Angel of Death and her brand of mercy. He had seen men recover from a crushed leg or lost arm and continue to keep on despite the pain. The pain of memory; he shook his head at the foolishness of such an idea.

He would start working on the shave horse after a little rest in the breeze. He needed to make some pegs to hang tack in the stable and coats in the tavern. It was simple enough work but it took time. Everything took time. Too much of it gave him time to think, and that was dangerous.

Now there was that damned lawyer in town talking about how all the foreigners were stealing land from 'real' Americans. Johan smiled grimly at that thought. He had been one of the men that had helped build the place the man called his office. Now the little swine was telling people "no foreign hirelings or niggers" had anything to do with it. A man like that was what got respect in Minnesota? A man like that would twist the law to his own means, and his sort was the kind that saw Jeff Sipes walk free after murdering a woman and child. Was that the reality of American justice?

Johan ran a finger through his damp hair, it was thinning and growing noticeably gray. He saw a shape move in the window of the bakery and knew instantly it was Tisha. He smiled slightly. She was a good woman, and Mina called her a friend. That Mina liked and accepted her was all that mattered, and she seemed to be happy. Was there anything better than this in life?

Mina answered his question by sitting down on the soft grass beside him. She said nothing and just leaned back into his arms. Johan felt a smile cross his face as he set his pipe down and laid back on the ground with Mina beside him. Big white clouds moved lazily in the sky above them, the sound of the creek added to the comfort of the playful laughter of Freedom and the other girls.

"If there is a heaven it must be like this," Johan said quietly.

He felt Mina smile as she burrowed deeper into his shoulder. "I'll take it," she said.

Johan took a breath of her hair and chuckled. "People might talk if they saw us."

Mina laughed. "You would care?"

"No, no I would not."

Mina turned her head to better see Freedom and the girls. "You did right taking them in. Did you know they call you father behind your back?"

Johan was surprised at that. "Really?" He felt a bit of pride swell in his chest.

"Oh yes. They don't use the Sipes name anymore; ever. Now they call themselves the Steele sisters. No one disagrees."

"What about Tisha?" Johan asked.

"She calls me sister and you she calls brother," Mina said with a grin in her voice.

Johan laughed. "I expect that was quite some surprise to Ivan when he started courting her."

"He'll not call her a liar. Those two get along well and Ivan is a gentle giant. If Jeff Sipes were to return he would protect her."

Johan stiffened at the mention of Jeff Sipes. "He will not," he said quietly.

"I know. He will never show his face near here again." Mina said. There was a drowsiness in her voice.

Johan stared up at the sky and listened to Mina begin to breathe the steady breath of sleep. He ran his hand lightly up and down her arm and looked at the sky. Sipes was in hell where he belonged and there was no way he could claw or lawyer his way out of there.

But the woman... the woman. Who was she? Did it matter? Johan had no idea but the idea of that dead woman haunted him. As far as he knew a woman had never been hurt by him until...

No, it did no good to dwell on it. There was nothing he could do about it. The woman was dead and buried. He had failed to identify the woman when he had trailed the Sipes party. What would or could he have done different? Would it have been any better to have simply shot Sipes? The others likely would have hunted him, and either he or they would be dead, leaving the woman alone on the prairie. What good would that have been? A lone woman on the prairie among the Lakota and white men with the morals of a rat stood little chance of much — or any — kind of a life.

Mina snuggled deeper into his arm and Johan looked at the top of her head. Men had called her an angel before, and so she was. Men had survived the war due to her care and the Moenning family owed her as well. If she had not helped them when fever ravaged the family, no one would have, and those two farms would be empty today. He had brought Mina here and she had saved lives simply by being who she was.

Without the two of them here, the Sipes women would be dead today, frozen or beaten to death by that bastard Jeff. How many women had that dog hurt? At least he could hurt no one ever again.

But damn it all to hell, that woman haunted him. The image of her plain face would not leave him. At least he had done well by her in burying her right. She had been separated from Sipes in the grave and her spirit able to listen to his dying cries for mercy if it wanted.

Johan picked up his pipe and relit it, being careful not to wake Mina. She deserved her rest. Anything she wanted he would provide. She deserved nothing less. Without Mina, how many more might have died at his hand? How many innocent... he shook his head to chase away the thought. His mind wandered to Emmanuel. What would have happened to Emmanuel had they not stopped here? Would Emmanuel have gone west with Little Foot and died with him? Would his secret have been discovered among the Lakota or elsewhere?

He looked down at the girls at the laundry line. They had finished hanging the last of the wash. At least one of the boarders had paid them a few coins to do his laundry as there was a bright green shirt on the line he did not recognize.

Those three girls truly were beautiful. Freedom would grow to be a beautiful woman. Danielle and Sherrie would be wed in a year or less. The Moenning boys were strong men of good character. They would do well by each other. He envied them their young love and the life ahead of them. And Ivan... poor fool. Ivan was in love with Tisha and that poor woman had never experienced love. He was happy for the both of them.

He should have been content with this place, the business built here, and Mina. But he could not say when he had ever truly been happy. He had no idea what it was supposed to feel like. He looked at the raven black hair nestled against him and then to the sky. If this was happiness, he would gladly take it.

Murder Solves Nothing 1877

Crazy Horse and his warriors fight their last battle with the US at the Battle of Wolf Mountain in Montana, and Crazy Horse is murdered later in the year. A compromise elects Rutherford B. Hayes, leading to the rise of Jim Crow and the end of Reconstruction. Henry Flipper becomes the first black man to graduate from West Point.

Emmanuel wrung out the dishrag and looked at the clock on the mantle. It was well past midnight, and still hot both inside the tavern and out. It was time for the bar to close down so Emmanuel could get some sleep. When Johan came back down from checking on Mina and Freedom, it would be time for this Bois jackass to go home. If Emmanuel had ever seen a poster child for the need to avoid whiskey it was this big teamster.

The MacGowan brothers had just left and the place was empty but for this idiot. The man could barely stand and the walk back to the boarding house in town was a long one for a drunk man. Especially one as drunk as this fool. The plus side, it was warm enough for a man to comfortably sleep on the grass of a pasture or alongside the road.

The drunkard let out a loud belch, doing his best to make it as loud and obnoxious as possible then wiped a shirt sleeve across his bulbous nose. He had a long face with a greasy beard that he liked to comb into points... it looked foolish as far as Emmanuel was concerned.

The man had some education and was smarter than everyone around him, or so he said, and it was true, therefore as far as he was concerned everyone had better believe it. If they didn't, he'd berate or beat them into submission. Which action depended entirely on how big or tough the other person might turn out to be. The man was a bully, and frankly a coward. He was always careful to pick on those smaller than himself, and kept his mouth shut around Ivan or Johan. Emmanuel suspected the man was smart enough not to antagonize real fighting men. He'd been smart enough to stay out of the ranks, after all. According to him, all soldiers were idiots. Again, it had to be true because he said it was. Earlier he had called the

GAR an organization of losers and has-beens that was no friend to anyone. The reality was he should have said to 'just anyone.' Wannabes, stay-behinders, and never-have-beens like this gutless wonder, weren't welcome.

If you listened to the man, he was the best carpenter, shipwright, sailing captain, and college professor in the state, if not the whole country. Emmanuel suppressed a smile. While he might have done *some* of that, more than likely he was an utter failure at things and just got by with bluster.

Bois loudly spit on the floor. "Say, Ezekial. Any of those womenfolk upstairs single?"

Emmanuel scowled. "No, and you knew that the last two times I answered."

"Jus' making sure. That prairie nig woman is nice but the nig and her little girl is downright pretty. Think that Johnnie fella would take a gold eagle for her?" The man slurred.

Emmanuel saw red and before the thought to stop came to mind was over the bar and on him with an unconscious roar of rage.

The man let go a surprised grunt as Emmanuel bore him to the ground. His big head bounced nicely against the stone floor. Emmanuel grabbed him by the hair and proceeded to smash his head against the floor again then raised a fist to continue the work of teaching the bastard the error of his ways.

"You son of a bitch!" the man roared and threw Emmanuel off. Emmanuel landed painfully against the brass rail at the base of the bar but managed to scramble up quickly.

The Bois man was big, a third again heavier than Emmanuel. He was also quick, quicker than a man that big and drunk had any right to be. He stood and drove a strong right cross square into Emmanuel's ribs. Emmanuel let out a gasp of pain and heard the sound of ribs breaking. Emmanuel retaliated by kicking out wildly, catching the man in the right knee. He staggered back and fell backwards over one of the bar stools. His head caught the brass rail hard enough to bend it. Emmanuel failed to hear the ugly snap and wet thump that came with it.

Emmanuel staggered upright as pain stabbed outward from at least one broken rib and readied for the beating that was sure to come. The Bois man was a monster. Emmanuel was badly outclassed and knew it.

But the man on the stone floor did not move. Emmanuel just stood there breathing, again feeling the sharp pain from at least one broken rib, if not two or three.

The stairs let go their telltale squeak as Johan ran down them. "What the hell?" He stopped abruptly as he saw the body on the floor.

Emmanuel turned to Johan. "I don't..."

"Shut up." Johan snarled as he ran to the dead man. Emmanuel knew the man was dead. No man's head should be at that angle. Then the smell of spilled bowels reached Emmanuel. That could only speak of death.

"You stupid fool. You killed him," Johan hissed.

Emmanuel felt the jaw open and close silently. "I didn't mean to..."

"Are you hurt?" Johan demanded as his eyes settled on the hand holding the ribs.

"I'll be ok." Emmanuel said quietly while staring at the dead man.

"Bull roar. Go wake up Mina and tell her you need to be bandaged. She already knows you're a woman. Make sure not to wake Freedom, or so help me God I'll finish what this damned fool started." The words were savage, but Johan was speaking in a far calmer manner than Emmanuel would have expected. "I will clean up this mess. It is what I am best at."

Johan set the heavy corpse against the back door of the law office and smiled slightly. It would serve the bastard right having to explain why there was a man with a broken neck at his back door. He had to get moving, it would not do for him to be seen. It was only an hour or two till sunrise and people would be stirring soon.

Johan chuckled sourly. The sheriff and this lawyer were anything but friends. He might like to know what kind of questions would be asked when the body was found. The teamster Drummond Bois was a notorious bully who many knew had been paid to do some underhanded work for this lawyer in the past. That the lawyer kept a brick bat beside his door was also well known as the fool had bragged about how tough he was. That brick bat would leave a wound not that much different than the brass rail had and was heavy enough to easily break a man's neck. At least a dozen people could vouch that Bois had been drinking heavily last night. Maybe Bois went to have a chat with the gutless bastard... maybe, just maybe, this lawyer was going to have some explaining to do. The man lied for a living, could he talk his way out of this? Johan smiled slightly; he hoped not.

Johan walked the two blocks down to the livery stable, blessing the early morning fog that masked him at the same time as he cursed the damp for making his bones ache. He skirted around the edge of town so that he came at the open door of the livery stable from the direction of his inn. He made certain to stay in the shadows and watch carefully for any curtains that might move or any lights struck that would betray someone awake. As far as he knew no one stirred enough to see him.

Mina's boarding house was full to overflowing and Clayton Jeeves had not wanted his horse in the over-crowded stable. The man was leaving today, it would not hurt for Johan to bring him his horse. It might even garner him a little extra coin in thanks. Most importantly it was an excuse for him to be in town.

When Johan walked into the livery stable he saw the stableman, Eddy, feeding and watering the horses. "Eddy, what are you doing up this early?" Johan asked as the man poured a bucket of corn into the feed trough. The man should still have been sound asleep.

There was a slight stutter to his speech when Eddy spoke. It made the man sound faintly foreign. "That Mr. Jeeves, he paid me extra to feed his horse a poke of corn every morning. He said he be wanting to be leaving today."

Johan had not known about the request for corn. None would ever ask Jeeves if he was a fool. Horses preferred corn and it gave them a better bottom. A corn-fed horse would go farther than any grass-fed horse. As far as Johan was concerned that was a big part of how the US Cavalry had managed to chase down the Lakota under Crazy Horse.

"Is that Big Bois horse?" Eddy asked and Johan turned to look at the hitching rail in front of the saloon. The horse was loudly drinking from the water trough there, exactly where Johan had left him a half hour ago.

"Heh, he closed us down last night. He only left my place a couple hours ago. I did not think the saloon would be open that late," Johan said as he pulled out his pipe and began packing it.

"Big Bois must have been real drunk. He not allowed in there after he started that fight with the Surry brothers. Thought that was why he drank at your place."

Johan shrugged as he struck a match to light his pipe. "No one ever accused him of being over smart. He is likely sleeping it off at his room or in the ditch behind the saloon."

Eddy looked hard at that horse. Johan could almost hear the wheels turning.

"What does Mr. Jeeves owe you for taking care of his horse?"

"Oh... two bits should do it." Eddy said.

Johan handed Eddy the coin then added a nickel for good measure.

"I'll take him back to my stable. Save the man a walk at least," Johan said with half a grin around a puff of tobacco smoke. "Maybe make myself a little extra doing it."

Eddy was a good, hard working man. Johan had to admit he liked him, but many thought him simple. There had always been a good feel to him and Johan knew him to be far smarter than most.

"Emmanuel is leaving this morning. He has finally had enough and is heading west. Says he will make a try in Deadwood or maybe that new city by Fort Lincoln."

"I like Em-Emma- Emmanuel. He never waters my beer. I hope he does good out there," Eddy stuttered.

"So do I. He has said he wants a new start. He will do well I think," Johan said with a slight smile, knowing the stutter told more truth than Eddy realized.

"Johan, people call you a mean man. I think that's a lie. You, you got good women to take care of you. They like you. That's all I need to know, to know you ain't a mean man," Eddy said with his slight stutter.

Eddy was, what, sixty-five or seventy now? He'd been too old for the war and stuck out wandering for too long in the Dakota War. People said he had gone stupid because of what he had seen. Johan knew the man had buried a half dozen families and the Dakota had cut him a wide swath because they thought he was a mad man. He had piled two dead braves onto a travois and taken them to a village for their families to bury and that had only added to his mystique among the Dakota, and probably kept his hair on his head. He was the town grave digger and worked the livery stable. Many of the younger folk called him a simpleton. Johan knew better; Eddy was much smarter than he appeared. He was also the kind of man to think and ask questions. And he would ask those questions out loud.

Everyone knew about Johan and his morning walks. Eddy certainly did. So, seeing him was no surprise and picking up a horse for a boarder was as good a reason as any to be in town.

Mina bound Emma's bandage tight and heard her take in a deep breath of pain. Emma... it just wasn't right to call Emmanuel, Emma. Johan had told her last year, though she'd had suspicions of her own for quite some time, especially after Freedom had asked questions. But she had never quite been able to believe it. If Emma wanted to be known as Emmanuel, it was not her place to say anything.

"That really hurts, Mrs. Mina," Emma said through gritted teeth. Emma had a different voice than Emmanuel, lighter and with a slightly different pitch to it.

"Serves you right. Getting into fights for nothing. It was only ever going to be a matter of time before you killed someone or someone beat on you enough to discover you have curves," Mina said.

Emma went white with pain and possibly a touch of embarrassment. "Johan said Emmanuel needs to go away. I have to start new. I don't know how." There was both pain and fear in that voice. And it was Emma talking, not Emmanuel.

"Well then, Emma, we had best find you a dress and have you write Freedom a letter. She'll never forgive Emmanuel for leaving without saying goodbye."

"I… I wouldn't know how to say goodbye to her. She's the best thing that's come from my life." Emma said around a clear stab of pain.

"I doubt that. You helped build this place and you helped men come home from the war." Mina said as she opened a chest full of fabric. "You have to forget you know her or she'll know as soon as she sees you."

Emma said nothing as Mina held up a bolt of light-colored fabric. "This will do, Tisha, Danielle and Sherrie will have to know, particularly as I bought this fabric for Tisha. None of us have clothes that will fit you, we all have too many curves. We'll have to put together at least two outfits for you in a hurry, plus a set of stays.

"We're going to have to figure out how to change your hair to make it longer. You can wear a bonnet to start with, but people will wonder if they never see you without.

"You won't be able to work in the tavern, either. Too many old hands know Emmanuel, and some will see too much of him in you, even if you claim to be his twin."

Emma let a tear slide down her cheek and Mina brushed it away with a gentle hand. Emmanuel was gone now, forever gone and they both knew it.

Mina looked out the window at the morning fog below with the predawn light giving it a beautiful glow. There were a lot of questions and a lot of challenges ahead. They would be able to fool some of the people around here long enough for them to forget the surly barkeep but some would suspect something. Men like Korbel, Ivan and Vincent would figure things out but they would keep quiet. She knew them. What of the other regulars in the tavern? Emma would have to stay upstairs. Maybe Tisha could work downstairs for a while? No, she was too pretty and a drunk would get frisky with her, and then Johan would kill the man.

"Johan will have to hide your Spencer, too many know of your fondness for it. We'll have to figure out how to get you into town to check into the hotel there and put out the word you're looking for your brother. You can't just appear here out of nowhere."

Epilogue, 1890

I am a black woman born in 1864, at the end of the Civil War. My mother is Mrs. Mina Steele and my father... the tale of my father is an interesting story to tell. I have never called a man Father; Johan Steele filled that role, as did Emmanuel Lentsch. I was found - or rescued, depending entirely upon who you were to ask. I was then raised as the daughter of Mrs. Mina Steele and her husband Johan with the help of their good friend Emmanuel.

My mother and Johan made every effort to educate me and see me raised up into a better life. By the time I was ten I could speak three languages, and part of a fourth. I had gained a respect for the men and women working the land and living their lives, as well as an understanding of the difference between right and wrong. I also knew there was 'right' and 'what is.'

I have two women who call me sister: Danielle and Sherrie Moenning. They have married and each have wonderful children who call me 'Auntie.' Their mother Tisha has married but continues to work beside my mother and is her closest friend and confidant.

My mother insisted that I never stop learning, handing me a new book to explore as soon as I finished one. As a child I would disappear just as soon as my chores were done so that I might read. There was a favorite private place where I could be alone and no one would bother me. When Johan discovered my secret place, he would leave me little gifts that he believed I might like, or the occasional piece of candy.

The man never hugged me, or held me to his chest and told me that he loved me. To my knowledge he only ever told one person that he loved them and that was my mother. I cannot blame him for such. He was a hard man, and he did not think himself a good one. I cannot say if he was or not. My mother thought him one, and that is all that truly matters.

He tried to teach me the rifle and how to use a

blade. I refused, as I want no part of ending a life. My sisters had no such problem and were eager to learn. Until he died, he made certain they each received a new knife on their birthday and Christmas. If a knife could not cleanly cut paper it was not a worthy blade. When they married, he gifted each a rifle: "To put meat on the table or to convince some fool of the error of their ways," he said.

When I left home, Johan put a Smith and Wesson seven shooter in my hand and told me to keep it with me all the time. "It would be better

to have it and not need it than need it and not have it."
I never saw him carry or even handle a pistol but he showed me how to load and use it. Even though I hope never to need it, I keep it close by in his memory. If he did nothing else right by me, he did that.

Johan lived for my mother; never once in my life did my mother want for food or a roof over her head. My family never went cold in the winter or felt the lack of clothes, as there was always enough coin for what was needed, and I was happy. He never raised his hand to any of us. Can a child ask for more?

My mother taught me to cook, tend house, and to write in a readable fashion. She also taught me to think for myself, and that no one would do anything for me. I learned to do everything myself. I was taught to not expect help so I would not be disappointed when none appeared. If you are lucky, you will only be pleasantly surprised when someone does offer assistance.

Emmanuel was a broken man, he had lost his best friend in the Civil War and never truly recovered. As a child I would ask him to play his fiddle for me. I have since learned that I kept him from descending into total madness. Unfortunately, he was lost to us just a few weeks before his sister found him. He had thought her dead and may have blamed himself for her death. He headed west and word reached us that he had been found scalped somewhere near Jamestown, North Dakota. Emmanuel was a strange man whom I liked and maybe wished were my father. His twin sister Emma arrived just a few weeks before we received word of his death. She thought I was the finest thing in the world. She knew so much about me that I have no doubt there was a special connection between her and her brother. She is a strange woman, hurt by a loss she does not speak of, and one which my mother says I would not want to understand. Emma is so much like her twin brother that I can almost imagine them to be one and the same.

I left home in the summer of 1882 when Johan and Emma paid for my schooling to become a University Librarian at Lincoln University in Pennsylvania. Books are what I love more than anything in the world. They have been my whole life.

I cannot remember a day without a book and cannot imagine that I would ever wish for a day without one. In times of worry a book has kept me company, and when I was lonely it was always a book which made me smile.

I have been told that because I am black, I will never have the advantages of a white woman. I must admit that makes me smile as I am better read than most so-called educated people and have learned that I have a gift with languages. I speak English, French, Dutch, and some Lakota. None in my home growing up cared for the color of a person's skin; only what kind of person that they were and how they acted.

Johan and Emmanuel taught me the value of listening, and my mother and sisters taught me the value of a warm smile. So I have made my way in this world as a librarian. I have shared knowledge and education through the written word.

Any man who wishes to court me must live up to the expectations left me by Emmanuel, and those are large boots to fill. I fear no man might live up to them. Though to be honest,

I'm not certain I wish to be courted. What I have seen of men does not impress me.

Perhaps at the dawning of the new century our country will have changed for the better. A country where men and women are judged by their character instead of their sex and color of their skin.

Freedom Steele

About the creator...

Shane Christen is a budding level collecting nut. He is an admitted professional amateur who knows full well he has been bitten by the level bug. He has finished stage two and is embarking upon stage three of his self-described collector's metric.:

Stage 1: 1 for every day of the week.
Stage 2: 1 for every month of the year.
Stage 3: 1 for every week of the year.
After all, you need one to match your socks.

He has a wide ranging family of a father, wife and three children as well as several adopted sisters and nieces. There are a variety of other children who occasionally will call him dad or Uncle as well. May the lord have mercy on any future genealogist researching his family.

Shane continues to work in the retail and commercial security field as an Install Coordinator. He is also a board member and docent at a local military museum where he is known to ambush poor unsuspecting history buffs... He has a thing for American Civil War firearms, their associated musket tools, levels, Archimedes drills, axes, adzes and God only knows what next.

The good lord gifted him with the gift of gab. He failed to receive the gift of skilled hands for the use of fine tools. So he makes do with a personality that might have made a good teacher if he could tolerate the politics.

Bobbie, his angel and his wife tolerates his hobbies... so far. He is fond of showering her with gifts (aka blatant bribery) and reminding her how much he loves her lest he wake up dead some morning. After all 150+ year old levels work well for holding open cranky windows and old saws are even better at cutting down trees. If it works...

Other books by Shane...

Made in USA - Kendallville, IN
12400_9781945105005
05.03.2023 1328